DCS PALMER & THE SERIAL MURDER SQUAD

CASE 3
A KILLER IS CALLING

&

CASE 4
POETIC JUSTICE

Published by BSA Publishing 2017 who assert the right that no part of this publication may be reproduced, stored in a retrieval system or transmitted by any means without the prior permission of the publishers.

ISBN 978-1-9997640-2-9

BOOKS IN THE DCS PALMER SERIES (SO FAR)

BOOK 1. FUTURE RICHES

BOOK 2. THE FELT TIP MURDERS

BOOK 3. A KILLER IS CALLING

BOOK 4. POETIC JUSTICE

BOOK 5. LOOT

BOOK 6. I'M WITH THE BAND

All are available individually as e-books online or in double case paperbacks from your favourite book shop.

THE PALMER CASES BACKGROUND

Justin Palmer started off on the beat as a London Policeman in the 1970s and is now Detective Chief Superintendent Palmer running the Metropolitan Police Force's Serial Murder Squad from New Scotland Yard. Not being one to pull punches, or give a hoot for political correctness if it hinders his inquiries Palmer has gone as far as he will go in the Met. and he knows it. Master of the one line put down and a slave to his sciatica he can be as nasty or as nice as he likes.

The mid 1990's was a time of re-awakening for Palmer as the Information Technology revolution turned forensic science, communication and information gathering skills upside down. Realising the value of this revolution to crime solving Palmer co-opted Detective Sergeant Gheeta Singh a British Asian onto his team from the Yard's cyber crime unit. DS Singh has a degree in IT and was given the go ahead to update Palmer's department with all the computer hard and software she wanted. Most of which she wrote herself and some of which are, shall we say, of a grey area when it comes to privacy laws, Data Protection and accessing certain databases! Together with their small team of officers and one civilian computer clerk called Claire, nicknamed 'JCB' by the team because she keeps on digging, they take on the serial killers of the UK.

On the personal front Palmer has been married to his 'princess', or Mrs P. as she is known to everybody, for nearly forty years . The romance blossomed after the young *Detective Constable* Palmer arrested most of her family who were a bunch of South London petty villains in the 1960's. They have four children and ten grandchildren, a nice house in the London suburb of Dulwich and a faithful dog called Daisy.

Gheeta Singh lives alone in a fourth floor Barbican apartment. Her parents arrived on these shores as a refugee family fleeing from Idi Amin's Uganda and since then her father and brothers have built up a very successful computer parts supply company in which it was assumed Gheeta would take an active role on graduating from University. She had other ideas on this, and also on the arranged marriage her mother and aunt still try to coerce her into. Gheeta has two loves, police work and technology, and thanks to Palmer she has her dream job.

Combining the old coppers nose and gut feelings of Palmer with the modern IT skills of DS Singh makes them an unlikely but successful team. All their cases involve a serial killer and twist and turn through red herrings and hidden clues keeping the reader in suspense until the very end.

BOOK THREE   A KILLER IS CALLING

Chapter 1.

'It's just a mess Justin, an unholy fucking mess.' Professor Latin held the brain scan negative up to the light box on the wall of the New Scotland Yard Pathology Lab and shook his head in bewilderment. 'Imagine a ball of rubber dropped onto a fucking hot stove and this is what you would get, goo sticky fucking goo.'

'Hmmm.' Detective Chief Superintendent Palmer lent nearer the light box as he fumbled his spectacles from the inside pocket of his trade mark Prince of Wales check jacket and peered through them. 'So what causes this goo then? How does a human brain disintegrate into this kind of a mess?' He looked at Latin inquisitively over the top of his specs hoping for an answer that would at the very least give him some lead to pursue. He also hoped the answer would be without Professor Latin's liberal use of the *F* word as his second in command Detective Sergeant Gheeta Singh was with them.

'No idea Justin. Never come across it before. No fucking idea.' Palmer's hopes of an expletive free answer sank without trace as the professor continued. 'All I can tell you with certainty is that it's not drugs. We've done a complete gas and TL chromatography screening and nothing shows up, fuck all.'

Behind them DS Gheeta Singh took a call on her mobile. She caught Palmer's eye as she spoke quietly into it. He raised his eyebrows to the heavens anticipating problems as she clicked off and her expression told him it was not good news.

'What now?' He slipped his specs back into his pocket.

'I think we have another one Sir, he's been riding the circle line for a day and nobody noticed.'

Detective Superintendent Justin Palmer loved his job and being one of the 'old school' detectives at the Yard he treated his Serial Murder Squad like his own child. Now fast approaching retirement age, and having turned down early retirement repeatedly each time it had been offered by the powers on the fifth floor he was getting that buzz of excitement he always got as a new case unfolded. He knew that if he took an early retirement package the first thing the suits on the fifth floor would do would be to disband his squad and amalgamate it with the CID as a 'cost cutting' exercise. As far as Palmer was concerned that wasn't going to happen as long as he could stave it off.

Outside the Pathology Laboratory he removed his grey trilby and settled into the back of a squad car as Gheeta slipped in the other side. At least with the modern day squad cars he could stretch his legs a bit and relieve the stabs of sciatica that an old back problem had a habit of sending down his left thigh. The old style small Panda cars had been a source of continued pain and he had been glad to see the back of them..

'Right then,' he nodded to the driver. 'Acton Tube station, let's see what we have this time.'

The tube train had been backed off the District Line into the sidings at Acton Town station. Palmer and Singh stood in the carriage looking at the body of a young man slumped on a corner seat. To all intents and purposes he could just have been asleep resting against the heavy plastic partition beside his seat. But he was dead not asleep. There were no immediately visible signs of why he was dead, just a thin line of congealed blood that ran from his left down over the lobe onto his neck.

The British Rail Police Inspector was unmoved he'd seen it all before, many times before. The addicts seemed to find tube trains ideal for shooting up. He guessed it was because the trains all had a fairly quiet section to their routes once they were outside the hurly-burly of Westminster and the City. It was a section on the line where the lost souls of humanity could do the deed undisturbed. He had little doubt that the pathologist would find the tell tale needle marks and the dealers that rode the tube like parasites in a giant worm would now have one customer less to feed off.

'Usually vagrants or college kids, unusual to get one like this'

'Like this?' Palmer was interested.

'Yes a normal everyday looking chap. Smart dresser too. His personal effects indicate he was a bank worker in the city, odds on it's a Charlie OD. Usually is.'

'Maybe,' Palmer nodded. 'We will see once the autopsy is done.'

Sergeant Singh had noted Palmer's reluctance to say anything about the other three bodies already stored in the Wandsworth Police Morgue. Three bodies that all had the same trace of blood from the ears. According to the pathology reports none of them had been killed by a cocaine overdose, or an overdose of anything.

The BR Inspector continued. 'We've got officers going round to his work place and home now.'

'Right,' Palmer was glad to hear that, it meant he didn't have to spare any of his team to do it. 'Keep me up to date won't you please. My Sergeant will check in with you later for all the details, name address and so on.' He squatted and looked carefully at the dead man's ear and exchanged a knowing glance with Sergeant Singh.

Sitting in the back of the squad car travelling at less than walking pace in London's rush hour traffic wasn't Justin Palmer's favourite way of spending the afternoon but it did give him a chance to recap on the case. 'So that's four now Sergeant and we've not got the faintest idea why any of them are dead. When do we get the biopsies back from the Maudsley?'

Professor Latin's Forensics team had taken mouth swabs and blood samples from each of the three previous victims and sent them over the Thames to the Tropical Diseases Laboratory at Maudsley Hospital in Camberwell. It was a long shot but you never know, the victims may have had contact with a friend or a friend of a friend returning from the tropics with a virus.

'They should be back tomorrow guv. So they said anyway. Can't be a disease though can it?'

'Well if it is and it's catching we've probably got it. Not a very nice thought eh?' He shifted uneasily in his seat.

'No not very nice thought at all, thanks for sharing that guv.' Singh took in the seriousness of his remark.

'But,' Palmer threw her a reassuring smile, 'three victims in five weeks and none related to each other by family or work doesn't point to a nasty little bug flying around does it eh? And their nearest and dearest would be dropping like flies as well by now if it was and they haven't, but there has to be a connection between them somewhere, there always is.' He sighed loudly and settled back in the seat. 'I wouldn't mind a nice little bug to wipe out some of this traffic right now, I thought this congestion charging fiasco was going to clear the London streets and get the traffic moving?'

The driver gave a sarcastic laugh. 'Ha! It cleared off the Mayor's budget deficit Chief, that's all it did, traffic's just as bad if not worse.'

Palmer smiled. 'Ah yes but I bet it also gave our wonderful Mayor a pot of cash so he can keep the rates down and get re-elected. Never take a Politician at face value Constable.'

'I never thought of it that way Sir.' The driver nodded as it sank in. 'The crafty bugger.'

'You can bet the Mayor thought of it that way.' Palmer learnt a long, long time ago that nobody in public life ever did anything for the public good, only for their *own* good.

DS Singh smiled. Palmer's sarcasm amused her. He had a way of making people look at things differently. He's impressed on her a long time ago to never take anything at face value there's nearly always an ulterior motive behind the face. Or maybe he was just a grumpy old man. She checked the emails on her laptop as they came to another halt in the traffic in the Strand. Nothing important, just her aunty asking if she'd spoken to *'that nice young Indian businessman whose telephone number I gave you'*.... Soon, very soon, Gheeta would have to have an almighty row with her aunty and with her mum about arranged marriages. She grimaced at the thought of it. Generation gaps…culture clashes… the world had changed so much in the last few decades that some of the older generation were having trouble keeping pace with it. Mum and aunty being two of them. She turned her mind back to the case.

'You want to get a team meeting on this one guv?'

'No not yet,' he said and thought for a moment. 'I'm not really sure which way to go with this case as yet. Just keep putting all the information on the victims into the computer programmes as it comes in and see if we can get any matches.'

Chapter 2

Several of the hierarchy at New Scotland Yard had raised worried frowns when Palmer had plucked this novice WPC Gheeta Singh from the West Central street beat and given her half his operational budget and a free hand to bring in computers to his Serial Murder Squad office. But Palmer was a wily old fox and forty plus years in the Met. had honed his ability to pick out winners early on. He'd first been impressed with WPC Singh's IT aptitudes when she was able to re-programme his crashed HOLMES data base terminal in half an hour. A job the outside contractors usually had two people working on for three days at six hundred quid a day. At that time he didn't know Gheeta Singh was a university graduate in IT and Computing, or that she privately considered the Yard's systems to be very outdated and vulnerable. Her parents had brought the family into the UK fleeing Idi Amin's Uganda and had set up a technology business now run by her three elder brothers. Her father had steered her education through technical college and university grooming her to take a lead role in the family business but Gheeta's heart was set on police work from an early age and there it was to stay. And of course, as with most daughter father relationships, dad gave in. When Palmer had seconded her to his unit for a three month trial and let her range free over all the systems in his team room she was in her element. Upgrading, creating shortcuts, rewriting and deleting programmes, adding new ones and generally kicking the systems into the 21st century. After just one month Palmer pulled the necessary strings and the move was made permanent. That was four years ago. Singh was now a Detective Sergeant and Palmer knew she was the obvious one to take his role when he finally succumbed to retirement in a year's time. Well Mrs Palmer thought it was to be in a year's time but Palmer had no intention at all of hanging up his brain and becoming an assistant gardener to Mrs P in one year's time, or in five years time come to that. No, retirement was not a pleasing thought to him. Mrs P ran the house and garden with military precision and he generally felt he was in the way if he took so much as a day off work and usually spent most of it finding excuses to go out. And even his faithful dog Daisy drew the line at being dragged out for *five* walks a day even though she was a Springer with the excess energy of that breed.

At New Scotland Yard they signed in and climbed the stairs to the fourth floor offices which housed the Serial Murder Squad and went straight into the team room. This was a large open space room with all Singh's computers and terminals along one side on a work surface and various tables and chairs scattered around the rest of the room like a wedding party aftermath. It used to be the old canteen before the modernisation of the Yard and Palmer always got a well remembered whiff of early morning bacon sandwiches that had permeated the walls over the years every time he came into the room. Too many early morning bacon sandwiches according to Mrs P who worried about his expanding waistline. He removed his trilby and jacket and slung them on a handy table next to where his civilian operator was working a terminal.

'Claire, are you still here? Your hubby won't be pleased.'

Sergeant Singh had first met Claire in the admin typing pool and done a 'Palmer' on her having had her transferred as administration clerk to the team after noticing her reading Computer Weekly on her lunch break rather than the usual Hello or NUTS. A chat over coffee had yielded the information that Claire was doing an evening IT course and was something of a computer 'nerd'. She turned to greet them as they entered.

'Yep, still here I'm afraid Sir, married to my job.'

'Very commendable but I don't think your old man will appreciate it. Can't have the Yard cited in divorce papers.'

Gheeta unloaded her laptop from her shoulder and sat on the chair next to Claire. 'Anything?'

'No nothing at all. I can't understand it all we've got that ties the victims together is the way they died. Those blood trickles from the ear. It's like somebody just picked them out at random and zapped them with something.'

Palmer spoke, 'Could well be that's exactly what happened, random killings. Our killer gets up in the morning and has the urge to murder so out he goes and kills the first unsuspecting poor blighter he can without being seen. An empty tube train carriage is ideal. He does the job and hops off at the next station. Anybody getting on the carraige would think our victim was just sleeping. Is the final pathology report thru yet?'

Claire shook her head. 'No Sir, I'll chase it in the morning.'

Gheeta sensed a lilt to Palmer's question. 'What's your interest it that report guv?' Always 'Sir' in public 'guv' in private, 'You've an idea haven't you, I can tell, what are you expecting it to say?'

'Nothing really,' Palmer sat and tipped a chair back against the wall as his feet clattered up onto a table, 'but for blood to run there has to be a wound so I just thought they might find a needle hole or something inside the ear.'

Singh nodded. 'Yes but it's not very likely that the victims would allow somebody to push a hypodermic in their ear is it guv? Not going to sit there and say carry on old chap help yourself are they?'

'Not very likely at all *if* they knew it was being done Sergeant but what about if they *didn't* know it was being done?'

'How do you mean?'

'Well, maybe the killer chloroformed them first, just an idea.' He swung his feet down, got up and crossed the room to stand in front of the case progress wall board. Across one wall of the team room Palmer had a long wide plug board for updating the crime trail as it unwound. An *aide memoir* that he could ponder like a grand master ponders over a chess board before making the next move. The three victims' pictures and crime scene photos were all that graced it at present. Palmer pointed his finger at the first victim's set of photos. 'Hannah Robson, non descript housewife, 32 years old, just done the weekly shop and then drops dead in the front seat of her car in Asda's car park. A busy car park so we can assume that if she were attacked in any way she'd have shouted and it would have been noticed. Not a weak lady far from it, in fact just come from her twice weekly gym work out. Very capable of defending herself if need be. But, looking at it from another way, she's just come from the gym so she's tired, and now she's done the weekly shopping as well so she slumps into the car and, don't forget it was a very hot day, she takes a nap.'

'And mister X the killer comes up with his needle and injects?' Gheeta wasn't convinced.

'Could have, why not?' He pointed to the second set of pictures. 'Victim number two Samuel Haines, schoolboy, sixteen, getting his books together in his room at 7.30 in the morning and then, when mum goes to hurry him up, there he is, dead.'

'So where did the killer come from?'

'With Samuel I don't know.' He shook his head, 'I just have no idea...but with Arthur,' Palmer moved to the third victim's pictures, 'With Arthur I do. Arthur McGann was in a late night launderette, bachelor boy Arthur is doing his own wash, eleven at night...round and round goes the tub...Arthur is sleepy and dozes off.'

'Enter the killer.'

'Yes.' Palmer swung round and faced them putting his hands in his pockets. 'And the same with our chap on the tube train. He just dozed off. See it all the time on the tube.'

'And the killer injected him in the ear without waking him and what about the other passengers?'

'We don't know that there were any. If the killer is out looking for a victim he's going to be in no hurry and wait his chance. After all, any victim will do. All he has to do is bide his time until fate presents him with one which it did. So the answer to your original question about my interest in the Pathology Lab report is really two fold. Are there any puncture marks inside the ears of the victims and, if so, is there a foreign substance in that *goo*, as professor Latin calls it that used to be their brains?'

'That *fucking* goo guv.' Singh did a passable professor Latin impression highlighting the swear word.

Claire laughed. 'Been to see the professor eh? Do you think his language is as bad when he's at home I can't see his wife standing for that?'

'She's worse than him.' Palmer had met her. 'East End girl and you know what their language is like.'

Claire smiled at the inference. Gheeta lived in the East End. 'What did he think was the cause of death?'

Singh shrugged. 'He didn't know.'

Claire shivered. 'Bit sinister isn't it.'

'It seems that way at the moment Claire,' Gheeta sighed, 'but it'll come together, always does.'

Palmer smiled, Sergeant Singh was coining one of his phrases. 'Sergeant you get more like me with every case. You'll develop sciatica next.'

'Cynicism more likely.' Claire shot him a sideways glance.

He chuckled. 'Coppers stock in trade Claire, cynicism, sciatica and optimism they go hand in hand with the job. And divorces too so you get off home young lady you've done quite enough for today.'

Sergeant Singh walked over and joined Palmer at the wall board. 'Be nice to have a murder weapon wouldn't it guv eh? Even a bullet or a knife wound just something to get working on. Got nothing yet have we. If pathology come up with no pin holes and no substance we've even less than nothing.'

Palmer nodded in agreement. 'We've got to find the link Sergeant, that little thread that common denominator that ties all these unfortunate people together. Somewhere there is a link. Always is just got to find it. More than likely it's staring us in the face right now. We can't see it for looking, but it's there. I'd bct my pension on it. It's in there somewhere, but where?'

Chapter 3

'Not a sausage.' Sergeant Singh ripped the fax off the machine. It was the following morning.

Palmer looked up from the mountain of papers on his desk. 'What do you mean 'not a sausage'? I don't want a sausage, I want a pinhole or a substance?'

'No pinhole no substance just nothing guv,' She said as she placed the pathology Lab report in front of him. 'Zilch.'

Palmer scanned the paper for a minute and wasn't happy. He read from it, '*Undetermined intrusion*, what does that mean then? We don't pay those lab boys to come up with nothing.' He read on. '*The disintegration of the lower left part of the brain in each victim was caused by an undetermined intrusion*'......in other worlds they haven't a clue, great...very helpful.' He put the paper down on his desk with the other papers.

'If there's nothing there to be found guv they won't find anything.'

Palmer acquiesced. 'Yes I suppose that's true....any joy on joe public in the tube train?'

'Mister James Fennel guv, clean as whistle....bright upstanding member of his local community, leaves a grieving mother and father and a vacancy at Lloyds Bank city branch.'

Palmer sighed loudly. 'This isn't good is it eh? Four bodies all killed the same way and no motive and no weapon. I'm beginning to believe in aliens now.'

'The truth is out there somewhere guv, just got to find it.' Singh turned on her heels and made for the door. 'Some old copper I used to know was always saying that, then he went off his head and started believing in aliens.'

She was out the door before Palmer's hurriedly aimed biro hit it behind her.

In the team room Claire was pinning up the James Fennel crime scene pictures as Sergeant Singh walked in.

'Good looking lad wasn't he?'

'Yes,' Singh stood beside her and gazed at the slumped body in the picture. 'Just looks asleep really. If you were on the train you wouldn't know he was dead would you? No wonder he was going round and round the circle line all day. Did you get a copy of the pathology report?'

'Yes, disappointing eh? Complete blank. Bet the governor was overjoyed at that.'

'He wasn't best pleased.'

The door opened quickly and Palmer stood there hurriedly putting on his coat, the glint in his eye was strong, the smile was back.

'Get your laptop Sergeant, we have lift-off. Some nutter has just phoned the Mayor's office and demanded a million quid or he'll kill a thousand people.'

Sergeant Singh slung the laptop strap over her shoulder and joined him. 'Is there a connection?'

'Oh yes…..he knew the locations of all four of our victims.' Palmer was smiling broadly now. 'Game on.'

The Mayor was not too bothered and carried on working through a stack of official papers with his secretary who was trying hard to appear unflustered as Palmer and Singh waited in his office for the Mayors IT department man to search through the telephone recording machine to find the right call and replay it. The PR man fumbled with the buttons on his jacket trying to think of way to spin all this to the Mayor's advantage if it went pear shaped. He fidgeted nervously as the in-house techie pressed the buttons on the machine trying to extract the ransom call from the other 3000 of the day.

'Is this going to take all day?' The mayor was getting impatient. A rather obese man with a shock of red hair his political career had languished in the doldrums until a surprise win in the Mayoral elections had elevated him to this important position. A position, salary, expenses and pension that he wished to keep and with an election coming up soon the last thing he wanted was some idiot wasting his time with a false ransom demand. So far all his promises about cutting London traffic and clearing the beggars off the streets and improving the public transport had come to nothing and the only success he could claim was ridding Trafalgar Square of pigeons. And all they'd done was to fly up the road to Piccadilly Circus and crap all over Eros instead. He hadn't formulated a final manifesto for the upcoming election yet although he knew he wanted to cut the household rates bill which was a sure fire winner but which unsuspecting department was going to have their budget plundered to pay for it? And how could he placate them? Probably have to promise some civil servant an MBE in the next honours list. The PM would push that through if it meant keeping the London mayoral seat within the party.

The techie was having problems isolating the ransom call and was looking for an excuse. 'There are 4000 calls a day on this machine and I've got find and then isolate your one from that lot mate. Not easy.' He pressed a button and a number showed on the LED display and the voice of Mrs Randels of 23 Peach Crescent, Brixton came through the speaker enquiring about waste collection after a bank holiday.

Sergeant Singh leant past him. 'Wrong sequence, here let me have a go. We have the same machines at the Yard.' She pressed the right buttons in the right order and the LED showed a flying decrease to '0'. 'Press the forward arrow when you're ready,' she said, smiled at him and stepped back.

The mayor, not known for mincing his words or for his diplomatic skills raised his eyes from the papers from the papers he was studying to the technician. 'I suppose you're somebody's son or nephew are you? Obviously you didn't get the job on ability.' He shifted his gaze to Palmer. 'You ready to hear it then Justin?' He was interrupted as his mobile rang on his desk. 'Shit.' He answered it. 'Yes…..ok…but I'm busy now for about twenty minutes so get them coffees and take them on a tour of the building or something all right? I'll be as quick as I can.' He clicked the mobile off and put it on top of his papers. 'Bloody union officials they think they can wander in and you'll drop everything for them. Sorry Justin where were we, oh yes, are you ready to listen?'

Palmer smiled. 'Thank you mister Mayor I think so.' He raised an enquiring eyebrow to Sergeant Singh who had taken a lead from her laptop and interfaced it thru a digital recorder box and stuck a small listening microphone next to the machine so that she would get a perfect digital copy of the call downloaded to her computer. She nodded to the technician, whose face was still a bright shade of embarrassed red from the Mayor's comment and he pressed the button.

They heard the operator take the call. 'Good afternoon London Mayor's Office how can I help you?'

An obviously distorted voice came from the speaker sounding like a Dalek. 'Do you record these calls?'

'We do sir yes.'

'Good, I've killed four people. A lady in the car park at Southfields, a boy in his home in Harrow, a man in the launderette Acton and one more on a tube train. All have a wound within an ear. I intend to kill one thousand more unless I get ten million pounds. I will ring you again in four days time at this same time with a little demonstration, goodbye.' The caller rang off.

'Hello?.......hello.' The operator tried to reconnect.

The recording clicked off. Singh unplugged her leads and stove them into her bag. The Mayor chucked his glasses on his papers and leaned back into his overlarge leather chair rubbing his eyes.

'Well Justin what have I got, a harmless idiot or potential mass murderer?'

Palmer shrugged his shoulders. 'Well Sir, hard to say for sure but who ever that was certainly knows more about the four murders than he would do if he wasn't involved.'

'Could have got all that information from the news papers couldn't he?'

'Most of it yes Sir, but the tube train murder hasn't been released to the press yet, nor the information about their ears having similar wounds. He couldn't know about that.'

'That is a bit worrying. So what do we do now then? Can't pay him, out of the question. Pay one and there'd be queue from here to Lands End.'

'Sit tight for the time being Sir. That's all we can do at present I'm afraid. We'll get a trace on the call and hope the chap's not covered his tracks too well.'

Sergeant Singh looked up from her laptop screen. 'It's a mobile Sir, not much chance of a trace result there.'

The Mayor was confused. 'Why not, mobiles have numbers and are registered aren't they? This one is.' He waved a hand at his own mobile phone on the desk.

Singh smiled nicely as she explained. 'You don't *have* to register a mobile Sir. Just buy it, put in a SIM card and away you go. If it's a pre-paid voucher phone you can buy call minutes at any supermarket or corner shop. We can get the number of the phone without any trouble and trace the call back to it and find the area where the call was made. But who owns it and where it is now, that is another matter.'

'Probably at the bottom of the Thames by now I shouldn't wonder,' added Palmer, 'or had its memory wiped clean, another SIM card popped in, and hey presto....new phone with new number, in which case it's totally untraceable.'

'Okay so what about his little *demonstration* in four days time?' The Mayor was worried. 'I don't like the sound of that.'

'No,' Palmer frowned, 'nor do I. Let's hope we get to him by then.'

Chapter 4

Sergeant Singh lay wide awake in her fifth floor
Barbican apartment looking across the bedroom and
out of the panoramic window to the dark sky above.
A few dark clouds reflected the orange red lights of
the city back to their source. She shifted her legs in
the bed as her mind pondered the day's work. They
really had nothing to go on. Just the phone call to the
Mayor's office and she felt sure that wouldn't yield
much.
A kiss on her shoulder made her aware that Mark, her
partner for the last 6 months, was stirring beside her.

It was a long time since Palmer had a kiss on his
shoulder. These days after 38 plus years of marriage
he was lucky to get a peck on the cheek when he left
for work in the morning. It wasn't morning it was
very late night as Palmer stood looking out of his
bedroom window past his back garden and over the
trees and grass of Dulwich Park. Everything seemed
coated in a blue hue from the moonlight falling from
the clear night sky but he could see dark clouds
forming in the distance. Behind him in the king size
double bed Mrs P slept soundly. The luminous hands
of his bedside alarm said two ten. She would have
been asleep since eleven. Creature of habit was Mrs
P and eleven was bedtime come hell or high water.
Palmer had once tried to work out the number of
times in a year that he actually got to bed at the same
time as her. But after he got to three months and had
only made it add up to five days he gave up. Thirty

eight years married to a copper was a long time and he fully appreciated the sacrifices Mrs P had made with the words '*I do*'. He often wondered whether she had regretted it. Oh well, three children and eight grandchildren kept her life full. Serial murders with no clues kept his life full. But now the adrenalin was flowing, this latest killer had broken cover with his phone call. Yes he thought, the game was now on. He unintentionally said it out loud as he made for his side of the bed. 'Game on.'

'Oh no it isn't not tonight Justin,' Mrs P was still just about awake. 'I've got a WI coffee morning tomorrow and need my sleep so behave yourself. Anyway you know it sets your sciatica off. Night-night sweetheart.'

Chapter 5

'What sort of demonstration?' Claire typed away as she asked Sergeant Singh the question.

It was the next morning and Singh stood coffee in hand at the wall board hoping for divine guidance to give her a lead.

'I don't know Claire I wish I did but it's got to be another murder hasn't it eh? Just to prove he can do it. To prove he has the power.'

Claire stopped typing and swung her seat round. 'God that's some sort of challenge to the boss isn't it? *I'm going to murder somebody on such and such date stop me if you can.* Bit of a heavy scene.'

'Yes very heavy and not much we can do to stop him at the moment.' Singh walked to the work surfaces that ranged along one wall and where four state of the art computers were sifting and sorting every little detail they could find on the victims. She patted one lovingly as though it was a pet. 'Come on you little darling, spill out a match….in fact spill out anything.'

Sergeant Singh had worked all the hours God gave her for six months when Palmer had passed her his office budget and told her rather bluntly. 'Get what you need, do what you want to do, but make it work.'

She'd taken the basics of every computer matching program from Find Your Perfect Partner to the Formula One racing optimum fuel mix programs, ripped them apart and rebuilt them on top of the rather tired Police issue HOLMES program software. They were programmed to look and find the slightest match between subjects. Everything was printed out….if two victims had the same tooth capped it would pick it up. But more usefully it picked up when they had the same friend or same tastes in food or had been to the same primary school or….well just about anything that Palmer could send his team out to probe and prod in the hope that underneath that insignificant morsel was the key that he was looking for to break a case open. The success rate had stunned Palmer. Not one to fight shy of new technology he had prayed it would come up with the goods on a couple of seemingly hopeless dead end cases so that he could justify his spend to the suits on the fifth floor. More than that would be a big bonus. Not only did he get more, much more, but the side effects were enormous. The case solve time was cut by seventy percent and the clear up rate for his department since the computers came in was a perfect one hundred percent. But of course the flip side of the coin was that along with the plaudits came the extra work load! Palmer was an old style copper who solved crimes and it was just fate that as a young Detective he was put on a couple of serial murder cases that were going nowhere and had cracked them. In so doing he got himself a reputation for the genre and now every unsolved serial murder in the UK landed on his desk. And usually after local CID units had finished with them they were as cold as ice.

Claire sighed as she checked the computers findings. 'Nothing coming out except that James Fennel….'

Singh moved over behind her. 'The tube train guy?'

'Yes. He had his mobile phone stolen.'

'Yes, I've had two pinched myself, big business now, usually two youngsters on a moped.'

'Yes but he had his stolen on the tube.'

'How do you know that?'

'Because I ran all the victims thru the mobile phone registered users databases to see if we could get a record of any of them phoning each other......' The printer beside her computer started to whir out papers.

'And?'

'Here, I've printed it out look,' Claire ripped the paper from the printer and laid it on the desk in front of them. 'They all had mobiles and none have made any calls since their murders, which is what you would expect of course, except Fennel's. His mobile went mad on international calls for a period of six hours after the time of his murder then the credits ran out and it went silent.'

'Usual scam then eh?' Gheeta looked down the print out. 'Nick the phone and hammer it until you get cut off or run out of credits then slip in a new SIM card and flog it with a new number, easy money.' She picked up the print out. 'I'll see if the governor wants anything done with this. I bet he will. Probably have me tracing all the calls. Still, you never know. If the killer took it I don't think he would be so daft as to phone home, but you never know.'

Sergeant Singh was right. Palmer had her trace every call made on the Fennel mobile. They all terminated in India or the Caribbean which underlined her assumption that some opportunist phone thief had probably seen Fennel slumped in the corner seat of the tube and thinking he was asleep had stolen the mobile. Obviously being a professional thief he would have had it, and any others he'd managed to steal, into a back street phone shop within hours and been charging half the normal cost for overseas calls to customers who weren't bothered about the phones history, just the half price calls. All the calls he made prior to those checked out to be Fennel's family or work numbers

Chapter 6

The Mayor wasn't very happy. The four days were up and Palmer's team had taken over his office in anticipation that this serial killer would keep his word and phone. He really didn't need this. He was desperately trying to think up some scam to have the public praise him and landslide him back into office and now he'd got an idiot killing his electors and demanding ten million to stop.

'I thought you would have nailed him by now Justin.'

Palmer smiled a *'you do your job and I'll do mine'* type smile. 'Not a lot to go on mister Mayor, random killers hold all the cards till they make a mistake.'

The voice print analysis had come back negative, it didn't match any others on file. The recording had been put thru the machines and the distortion taken out to give the caller's real voice as far as possible and then sent for profile analysis. It came back as London, educated male and that was about the extent of the profiler's report. Palmer had remarked sarcastically how useful that was as it cut the suspect list to about 7 million. Technology he could see the benefits of, psychoanalytic profiling he couldn't. He looked round the Mayor's office which now resembled the inside of GCHQ at Cheltenham. Banks of terminals, high speed tracing equipment, direct lines to phone number data banks and several of the Met's technicians that Sergeant Singh had pulled in for the operation. Singh was doing a last minute check on the phone amplifiers. All was ready, if the killer called they'd have a fix on his position within 80 seconds which might be totally useless because ransom type phone calls usually come from unregistered mobiles or public pay phones in busy pedestrian areas that a patrol car couldn't get to fast. Railway stations, shopping malls, airport concourses and the like were usually favoured.

The Mayor strummed his fingers on the desk and tried to look unworried by the whole affair. His secretary fumbled nervously with her blouse collar and the PR man was thinking that the best way out this if it did all go wrong was for the Mayor to make a point to the press about his faith in the police and confidence in their methods, thus subtly passing the buck off his desk to theirs.

The Mayor stretched his arms above his head and sighed. 'Looks like Microsoft's head office in here eh? Hope the bastard phones after all this trouble.'

Palmer was confident. 'He'll phone alright Sir; I'll put my mortgage on it. This one is a very clever sod I'm afraid he's got everything planned out and so far his plan is working well for him.'

The loud ringing of the desk phone amplified through the speakers cut through the room. Everybody stiffened. Singh put her hand by the receiver ready to lift it for the telephonist to take the call. She looked at the telephonist who was quite pale.

'You all right?'

'Yes, I'll be fine.'

'Ok just be normal, just like taking any other call.' She looked to Palmer who nodded. She raised the receiver for the telephonist who took it.

'Mayor's Office how may I help you?'

The unmistakeable distorted voice came over the speakers loud and menacing. *'I know you are surrounded by police and I know they are tracing this call so you have precisely 4 seconds to put the Mayor on the line before I ring off. ...one......'*

Singh look anxiously at Palmer whilst around the room technicians were flicking switches and hitting keypads in the race to pinpoint the call.

'...two...'

Singh held up four fingers to Palmer and mouthed. 'Four seconds not enough time.'

Palmer nodded he understood. He looked to the Mayor and mouthed. 'Keep him talking.'   The mayor nodded and stepped towards the telephonist.

'....three...'

The Mayor took the phone on Palmer's signal. 'This is the mayor speaking who are you and what do you want?'

There was nail biting silence and Palmer wondered whether the line had dropped out and they had lost him. Then the speakers gave forth again with the Dalek voice.

'Have ten million pounds ready to be switched into a foreign bank account by this time in four days.....'

The Mayor tried to interrupt. 'I won't be able to do it in....' But the voice carried on regardless.

Singh looked at Palmer. 'It's a pre-recorded message Sir. Tape probably.'

The voice continued as Palmer nodded that he understood. *'.........should that money not be in the account within 24 hours of you being given its location and number then at least one thousand people with die.......one thousand people at least.........'* The voice paused for effect. *'And now for my demonstration I promised you...I will count to ten....one....two...three.....'*

Proceedings were briefly interrupted as the Mayor's mobile rang on his desk. The Mayor waved a hand to his secretary to take the call. She picked it up and whispered, 'Hello?' It was the last word she ever spoke. Silently like a ship slowly sinking beneath the waves she dropped to the floor the mobile spilling from her hand and sliding away. The distorted voice counted on as Palmer and Singh reached her. He checked her pulse as Singh started CPR, nothing, no heart beat. Singh moved the secretary's head face up to start mouth to mouth. They both spotted it at the same time and stopped in their tracks. It wasn't much...but there it was, a tiny scarlet glistening trickle of blood running from her ear. The Mayor was at his office door shouting down the corridor for medics.

The voice on the speaker carried on.

'....eight...nine....ten......I think I have made my point by now haven't I? Ten million ready for four days time.' The phone clicked off leaving a hum from the speakers. Palmer crossed quickly to the technicians.

'Get anything?'

One of them nodded negatively. 'Nothing sir.....no fix....he's a clever sod.....routed it through ISDN internet lines and proxy servers.'

Palmer looked to Sergeant Singh for a translation although he knew what she would tell him but she was still trying to get life back into the secretary and handing the CPR over to the newly arrived medics. She got up and crossed over to him.

'Basically Sir he's got the recording set up somewhere on a timer and set it to ring this number using an internet modem connection which means he can program the call to go through lots of different servers before it gets here. Sort of scenic round the houses route so to speak.'

'Can we still trace it back to the source?'

'We can try but my bet is he's using proxy servers, the sort of places you go to get an encrypted pseudonym and be untraceable if you wanted to surf the kiddy porn sites and not be found out. They're big business now and mostly sited in Russia and Eastern Europe, unlicensed and unaccountable. If he's routed the call through three or four of them forget it we'll never trace him.'

The paramedics tried in vain to revive the Mayor's secretary and after a while they shook their heads, covered her over with a blanket and took her away on a stretcher. The pathologist was called.

The Mayor sat back at his desk visibly shaken and silent for once. He reached down to retrieve his mobile. Palmer's strong hand caught his wrist and stopped him.

'Sorry Mayor, we'll need that, we may have better luck tracing that call than we have with the other one.'

'He meant to kill me Justin,' The Mayor spoke quietly. 'I'd normally have taken that call. It should be me under the blanket. Jesus!'

'Well, if we don't get lucky soon you might need another hundred thousand blankets.'

The Mayor took in the gravity of the situation. 'I'll pay the little shit.'

'And when he comes back for more will you pay him again…and maybe again after that?' Palmer spoke sense and the Mayor knew it.

'Okay I'll pay him the first lot and you can follow the money and get him that way it should be easy enough to trace through bank to bank account transfers.'

'Easy enough over here Sir, yes, but what if the bank he transfers it to is Swiss? Took the victims of the Nazis sixty years to even get an acknowledgement their stolen money was in a Swiss bank let alone get it back. Lots of safe havens in the world for illicit money if you've enough of it…. and I think ten million is well enough.'

'So what do we do?'

'We hope four days is enough time for us to dig out a lead on the bastard and close in. That's what we do sir. And at least we know we're not looking for a hypodermic needle anymore.'

'Sir,' Sergeant Singh caught his attention. He joined her and the technicians who were engrossed looking at a green monitor screen on which a series of zigzags moved up and down the tail zagging to join the head and repeat the move.

'Pretty patterns eh?' The screen meant nothing to Palmer.

Gheeta explained. 'It's called a 'mouse trap' Sir. Our killer certainly knows what he's doing. The call was routed through proxy servers in Eastern Europe and Indonesia and then routed back on itself. Once the call was terminated it's like a hall of mirrors, each trace just sends you back to the last one and you basically go round in circles retracing your steps time and time again. It's a favourite ploy of some internet web sites so you can't leave them, only way to bust it is to turn off. Do that and you lose the whole thing.'

'Is there any way we can get to the original source of the call?'

'No Sir, no way.'

Chapter 7

The high panelled corridor of the Defence Ministry echoed Palmer and Singh's footsteps as they followed their uniformed escort who strode quickly along it. Palmer had no idea why Assistant Commissioner Bateman had called him urgently up to the fifth floor at the Yard and told him he was to go over to the Defence Ministry immediately and have a meeting with Lt Commander Layne. Their escort paused outside a door marked Navy Private. His loud knock was answered by a muffled '*enter*' from within.

Inside Lt Cmmdr Harry Layne rose from behind his enormous boardroom desk and with hand outstretched beamed at Palmer as they entered.

'Justin you old fox how are you?' Their hands pumped. 'How's the lovely Mrs P eh? Still wasting her life on you?'

'Hello Harry, we are both fine thank you, and your lot?'

'Yes, all okay thanks, offspring all fled the nest now of course, same as yours. Sit down, sit down.' Palmer introduced Sergeant Singh who was never really surprised at Palmer's contacts. He seemed to be able to produce somebody who knew somebody who could help whenever they floated into new uncharted waters.

The Commander smiled at Singh and motioned them both towards large comfy chairs and retook his seat behind the desk and offered an explanation.

'Justin, or should I say DCS Palmer and I both started our respective careers about the same time

Sergeant and at every damn management course I went on there he was, usually disrupting them by asking sensible questions which of course you mustn't do, ha-ha,' He giggled like a child at the memory. 'We had some damn good times didn't we Justin, damn good times. Didn't do one stick of good for our management skills but certainly honed our pontoon and drinking skills!'

Palmer gave an embarrassed smile. Day one of his *'four days'* given by the killer was coming to its end and he wanted to get on, not chat about old times.

The Commander must have learnt something from one of their courses as he picked up the serious vibes from Palmer and settled down to serious work. He thrust sheets of paper over the desk to each of them. 'Sign those please.'

Palmer took out his pen. 'Official Secrets Act?'

'Yes, the information you want is embargoed I'm afraid.'

Singh followed Palmer and turned to the last page and signed it. I was obviously just a usual formality although her curiosity would have liked her to read the whole thing, all fourteen pages of it.

The Commander reached and took the papers back, countersigned them and put them into a drawer under his desk. 'Right that's out of the way so now bring me up to speed on what you've got so far then on this killer who's holding the Mayor to ransom?'

Between them Palmer and Singh went through the case from the beginning to the unfortunate incident in the Mayor's office. When they had finished the Commander sat back with long sigh.

'The man you're looking for is George North.'

Both Palmer and Singh were a trifle stunned by this. Both thought it prudent to stay silent and await the explanation for such a direct statement.

'I want to bring in one of our security people to give you information on North and work with you on the case. He knows North inside out, any objections Justin?'

Palmer shrugged. 'No we could certainly use some help on this one.'

The commander pressed his desk intercom. 'Would you come in now please.' He took two large photos from his desk and passed one each to Singh and Palmer. 'That is George North.'

The photos showed a uniformed naval officer, late middle age and serious looking.

A side door to the room opened quietly to admit a young man also in Naval Officer uniform who crossed silently to the desk and stood beside Layne. Only when she looked up from the photo towards him did Sergeant Singh's heart miss a beat.

The young officer was her partner Mark. They looked at each other. Neither the Commander nor Palmer, who was committing George North's face to his memory, noticed the sign of recognition on her face.

Layne did the introductions. 'This is Mark Randall, he's handling this case from our end. Mark this is Detective Sergeant Singh and Detective Chief Superintendent Palmer, Serial Murder Squad New Scotland Yard.'

They nodded to each other and smiled the perfunctory smile as Randall sat down in a chair alongside them. Palmer guessed he was MI6.

The Commander ran over the brief details of the murders for him. 'Looks like we have the proverbial 'loose cannon' out there eh?'

Randall nodded yes and added. 'What he has in his armoury is far more dangerous than any cannon.' He paused to decide where to start. 'George North is, or was, one of Portland Down's top boffins. He was seconded to there from AT&T research twelve years ago. At AT&T he was team leader researching wavelength possibilities on very high ultra frequency radio bands for communications. He was years ahead of anybody else in his field and he knew it. He came to us and said that the research he had completed had convinced him that he could make a people destructive weapon with NCD, no collateral damage. In other words he could kill an enemy inside buildings or vehicles without damage to that building or vehicle using a wavelength frequency signal. Now, replace the word vehicle with the word submarine or even aircraft carrier and you can see the ramifications of what he was claiming. Taking it to the maximum it would mean de-populating a big city whilst doing no structural damage leaving the infrastructure and means of Government intact.'

'By *de-populating* you mean killing the population?' Singh looked him straight in the eyes having regained her inner composure

'Yes I do.'

Palmer was having difficulty with the concept before him. 'This is science fiction isn't it? My God.'

'Science fiction has a habit of becoming fact over time Sir,' Randall was serious. 'North was only on the very first tentative experiments using UHF sound but his results were promising and he had an increase in funding and staff. He had found the wave band and pitch that could render the recipient inoperative...'

'You mean dead?' Singh said. Their eyes met again. Hers were cold.

'Yes Sergeant, dead.'

Palmer shifted in his chair. 'You mean that North had actually tested this bloody thing on humans and killed them?'

'I don't have that information Sir.'

'Yes you do.' Palmer wanted the facts he wanted to know what sort of weapon they were dealing with.

North remained silent.

The Commander came to his rescue. 'If it was tested Justin it would have been tested in the field, in a war theatre like Iraq or Syria.'

'I didn't think you'd pop down Morrison's and zap the bacon counter Harry. So what happened? Why did George North go off the rails?'

'Well,' Randall carried on, 'It's important to say at this point that North is not running around with a weapon of mass destruction that he can point at a building and kill everybody inside with. He does have the capability of killing by subjecting a person to the frequency but that frequency has to be delivered to the target at a very close proximity to the receiving diaphram.'

'Receiving diaphragm?' Palmer wanted clarity.

'The ear.' Layne explained.

'So delivery by phone would be just perfect.' Palmer's brain was racing.

'Yes Sir,' Randall nodded. 'And it would seem that's what he was showing you in the case of the Mayor's secretary, an example of his power. The other fatalities so far would have been caused by him calling a number by random.'

A thought occurred to Palmer. 'How do *you* know we are investigating these cases? The media don't know the victims are linked or how they were killed? We haven't released any information on weapon or method so how comes you've got all this information?'

Commander Layne took the question and gave the stock evasive answer. 'That's above our pay scale Justin.'

Gheeta knew how they knew. She'd always been open with Mark and had discussed this case with him as she had other cases previously. How could she tell Palmer that she was living with a Naval Secret Service operative and didn't even know it? All those evasive answers he had given her whenever she had asked about his work made sense now. She knew he worked at the Navy Desk in the Ministry but assumed it was a normal Civil Service position, not an intelligence agency position. Christ she felt stupid! She kept her head down and avoided eye contact with Mark.

Palmer thought for a moment and turned to her. 'Sergeant get Claire to find the last calls received on each of the victims mobiles. They would have been from North.'

Singh made the call.

Things were starting to make sense to Palmer now. 'So George North did a bunk with his little piece of equipment and decided to make it pay, but why?'

'The politics changed Sir,' Randall explained. 'To develop a delivery system that could deliver the required frequency strength to just a small two storey building from any distance would need a development budget starting around a hundred million and that's a conservative estimate. The problems would be enormous and the technology completely new. It would be comparable to NASA putting the first man on the moon. The time factor alone would be forty years plus so the decision was taken to mothball it.'

Palmer nodded he was beginning to understand this man North. 'And presumably mothball North as well?'

'Early retirement Sir, he took it but he didn't like it.'

'I can empathise with that.'

'Me too,' the Commander added.

Palmer thought for a moment, 'Okay, so where are we now? North just took off one day did he, just like that and disappeared? Spur of the moment decision.'

Randall smiled. 'No Sir, George North planned this. He planned it well in advance. He left the service and for a year did consultancy work for the big telecom companies. He kept his head down. We monitored him closely for six months as we do with all senior staff with privileged information that leave or retire. It's normal procedure nothing out of the ordinary. Then six months ago he took a holiday in Germany and vanished, until now.'

Sergeant Singh spoke. 'How did he get the weapon?'

Randall was embarrassed. 'He either took it with him when he left or got it out bit by bit over a period of time before he finally left. It's only a small box the size of a cigarette packet.'

'Well,' Palmer took a deep breath, 'we have got a bit of a situation on our hands then haven't we eh?'

The Commander rubbed his chin. 'I suggest Randall works with your team Justin. He has all the information and files on North and the technology involved. Anything else you want just ask me.'

'North's present whereabouts might help.'

'That we can't help you with I'm afraid. Not that we don't want to, we just have no bloody idea.'

Chapter 8

Gheeta was furious. 'I nearly died on the spot Mark. I could not believe it was you!'

Singh had arrived back at her apartment after checking in with Claire and calling it a day. Mark was already there. He sat on the lounge window seat as she took her shoes and uniform off in the bedroom. The anger in her voice resonating around the apartment.

He laughed. 'Fancy both of us working on the same case eh?'

Gheeta came through from the bedroom in sloppy jumper and jeans. 'Never mind that. Who the hell are you Mark Randall? Who am I sharing my life with? I meet you at a Security Conference, you tell me you work in security for the Armed Forces. I naturally think you're Military police.'

'I am sort of.' Randall was trying to make light of his subterfuge.

Gheeta was not having it. 'Military Police don't work in the advanced weaponry field Mark. Don't treat me like a fool ok? Military Police aren't on first name terms with Defence Ministry Naval Commanders. What are you Six or Five?'

'Pardon?'

'You, are you MI6 or MI5? I'd guess six.'

Mark rose and looked out over the Thames avoiding Gheeta's angry look. 'You'd guess right Six. Look Gheeta I'm sorry. You know what it's like. What you don't know can't hurt you.'

She took no notice. 'And where did MI6 find you? You don't apply for that kind of job. They find you. Where did they find you Mark? What is your past?'

'N14.'

Gheeta was getting even more angry. 'Jesus Mark! N14 is the lot that get the SAS out of trouble when they muck things up!'

Mark laughed. 'Well I never had to do that.'

Gheeta wasn't laughing. 'I need time to think this through. You've not been honest with me. You've used information I've given you. That's the only way your Commander would know Palmer was involved in this case. You should have told me you were involved with North as soon as I talked about the murders. You knew all the time he was doing it and said nothing to me, nothing. And if you are N14 then you will be on the watch lists of Iran, Iraq and any other country we in conflict with, Christ Mark I could be associated with you and probably have been. I could be on those lists now too! Being watched, files raised about me and my family! Fuck you Mark Randall, fuck you!' She turned and went back into the bedroom slamming the door behind her.

Chapter 9

Palmer stood in his shirt sleeves at his office window gazing down at the busy evening theatre crowds and tourists as they window shopped Victoria Street and took photos of each other beside the revolving Scotland Yard sign. His mind was miles away. Claire's results from the mobile phone companies had been just as he had expected. Each victim's last incoming call was from the same unregistered mobile. Yes they could give him the number of the phone but he knew full well he'd never find it after what Gheeta had told him about proxy servers. Cul-de-sacs. This case was full of them. And it was full of them because the killer was using technology he knew backwards and bending it to his advantage all the time. The SIM cards, the proxy servers, and the mouse traps this whole damn internet and mobile phone thing was going to give the criminals of the world a new dawn a whole new landscape of unregulated criminal opportunities to exploit. He was thankful he had got Sergeant Singh on board. He could use ten more like her. He sat to his desk and did his customary thing of leaning the chair onto its back legs and against the wall as he swung his legs up onto the desk. *So mister George North you're going to kill a thousand people are you? And just how do you propose to do that eh? Ring them all up and…………*Palmer's body froze…*yes…….yes indeed! That would be the only way he could do it…..but how?* He felt the adrenalin pump….*just how could he do it? How could he phone one thousand*

*people at the same time? He'd have to use the mobile
network somehow.* He reached for his phone.

Sergeant Singh was still angry, very angry. So angry
she was shaking a little and felt like punching Mark.
Not a sensible thing to do with a N14 man. She felt
that she'd been used. She had never felt like that
before, her defences had been breached by love. Was
it love? If it was it had turned very quickly into anger.
Why couldn't Mark have told her the truth about his
job? Didn't he trust her enough? She had trusted him.
That was a big mistake. They sat in silence in her
kitchen picking at a pizza she'd had delivered. She
wasn't in the mood for cooking. The silence needed
to be broken by one or the other of them. Her mobile
rang. It was Palmer.

'How would he phone a thousand people at once?'

'What guv?' Her voice was still a little shaky with
anger.

'You all right you sound out of breath?'

'I'm fine guv, just had a jog.'

'I should take it slower Sergeant if that's what it
does to you.....anyway this North chap has got to
phone a thousand people at the same time to put the
ultra sound what-sit down the phone to them hasn't
he so how does he do that? How does he ring a
thousand people at the same time?'

'I don't know guv.'

'He'd have to use a network wouldn't he? Key into
it and get it to do the ringing out. So how would he do
that?'

'I don't know guv I'll find out first thing in the
morning.'

'Okay, get that Randall bloke to help you. But don't give away too much….I don't trust him. See you in the morning. Goodnight Sergeant.'

'Goodnight guv.' She flicked the phone off. Palmer's words *'I don't trust him'* bounced around her head. Palmer was very rarely wrong in character assessment. She looked Mark straight in the eye her mind made up. 'Tonight you are on the sofa. Tomorrow you're out of my life. No 'ifs' no 'buts' I want you out of here tomorrow. We will work together on this case in a professional way only. Our personal relationship is ended here and now.' And she went back into the bedroom, shutting the door and slipping the catch on behind her as tears welled up.

Chapter 10

He glanced at his watch, half past midnight. Not too bad. He stepped over his dog Daisy who raised a lazy eye and wished he'd hurry up and go to bed so she could jump up onto the sofa which she was banned from for a comfy night. Mrs P was already in bed so the coast was clear if Palmer forgot to shut her in the hall.

'Know anything about mobile phones do you Daisy?'

The dog recognised its name but the rest was gibberish.

'No don't suppose you do. Mind you very high ultra frequency is more your line eh? You dogs hear things we humans can't don't you eh? A different world, amazing.' Palmer had long since understood that the human race knew very little about what was really going on in the natural world around it and on a 24 hour time scale of evolution had barely passed the one minute mark.

He went down the hall and into the kitchen for his usual glass of milk before bed. His mind tossing and turning the facts of the case like a mad washing machine. Nothing was clicking together…..none of the jigsaw pieces were fitting together yet. He'd read North's security file, he seemed an ordinary bloke with no hang ups. Well paid. Bit of a loner but many scientific types are, it goes with the job. Bit like a copper, twenty four hour thing…..your mind never leaves the office although you do. Palmer drained his glass and washed it before starting up the stairs. Daisy was up into the lounge and settled on the banned sofa before he'd reached stair three. But just how was North going to kill the people…..a thousand of them? He had thought that Sergeant Singh would have known or at least have had an idea of how it could be done with all her IT knowledge and he had been quite surprised when she hadn't. Even he knew that cold calling companies could dial out hundreds of numbers at once and talk to the first one who picked up. She hadn't seemed herself on the phone. He had a quick wash in the bathroom, cleaned his teeth and quietly entered the dim bedroom. Mrs P's shape took up her half of the bed. He hoped Sergeant Singh and that Randall bloke got some answers from the mobile networks in the morning. That had to be the key…he stopped in his tracks his shirt half off….of course it was! A smile spread across his face…of course it was…delivery…what had the Commander said, they'd shut down North's research because the technology required to *deliver* the weapon would take forty years to develop. No it wouldn't Harry my old mate ….no it jolly well wouldn't…..bloody North has worked it out already and was about to prove it! Fuck! The expletive left his lips by mistake. Mrs P stirred.

'I suppose that language means you've been with Professor Latin today. He's a bad influence on you.'

Chapter 11

'Through a mast, he's going to get the signal to his victims through a mast.'
Palmer looked up from his desk and the reams of paperwork he kept meaning to make a start on. Singh and Randall had entered his office and stood like errand boys returning with the goods. Singh motioned Randall to a spare chair and sat behind her desk lowering the laptop from her shoulder as she spoke.

'We've been to all three major players in the mobile network field and each one says the same. You have two methods of delivering a message to that number of people. One, all their numbers would have to be fed into a computer program which can then ring them all at the same time and relay the message, or two, you hot wire into the circuit at the point of delivery which is a telecoms mast and deliver the message from the mast to the company server which then forwards it individually in a split second to all the mobiles that mast serves. Or you can pick and choose numbers but that needs a lot of time programming at the server end and North wouldn't have the time or the access. He is going to hot wire his little box of tricks to a mast'

Palmer took a deep breath. 'Which means that if my or your mobiles were on that server we'd get the call?'

'Yes'.

'Why did North say he'd kill a *'thousand'* people bit then? That's a specific number.'

Randall explained. 'It's a ball park number Sir, but he's well, well out. The current estimate of the number of mobiles on a mast server is approx eighty thousand and each of the three major services come up with that same figure.'

'So if each mast is transmitting through its servers to about eighty thousand phones and there are three main networks tied into that mast's server then it's transmitting to about a   quarter of a million phones any given time?'

'Yes.'

'How many masts are there in London?'

'Well depends on what you call London…but let's take it as within the M40 motorway ring…fourteen thousand.'

'Fourteen thousand masts and North could choose any of them to wire in his little box of tricks?'

Randall nodded. 'Yes.'

'We can't possibly physically monitor all those masts guv.' Singh cupped her head in hands on the desk. 'We would need fourteen thousand bodies!'

Palmer thought for a moment. 'So we have to whittle it down then don't we to probabilities and possibilities, any ideas?'

Randall took his jacket off as civil servants tend to do to give a false impression of starting work and hung it over Palmer's on the coat stand which didn't go down to well. 'We have a clue Sir, North took consultancy jobs at three mobile companies when he left the service. But only one of those was a service provider. The other two were research companies working on circuit boards and internet viabilities.'

Palmer moaned inside at the word 'internet', some more opportunities for the criminal world no doubt.

'Which service provider was it?'

'GT....Global Transmitters.'

Palmer lent his chair back against the wall and swung his feet onto the paper mound on his desk. 'So an educated guess at this stage would assume North will use the GT signal to send his deadly call and kill enough people to scare the Mayor into paying the ransom. So he's going to somehow intercept the signal at a mast and push out his signal. How difficult is that?'

'Very simple guv, sorry.' Singh smiled apologetically.

'Would be wouldn't it.'

Sergeant Singh explained. 'It's all fibre optic cables each one thinner than a hair, and each one can carry up to ten thousand phone conversations. So all he has to do is open the box of tricks at the foot of the mast and divert the cable through his box of death and hey presto he's in. And, it's the same technology for all three major mobile networks so he could wire into all three at once.'

'Christ, he's certainly got the upper hand hasn't he eh? Any luck on tracing him yet?'

Randall shrugged. 'None Sir, every lead goes stone dead after he went to Germany.'

'Got it all planned hadn't he eh? No loose ends, the clever sod.'

The office phone rang. Sergeant Singh took the call.

'It's the mayor guv, for you.'

Palmer took the call on his line.

'Mister Mayor what can I do for
you?......who?.......have they?.......have they
indeed?........yes, yes.......say about an hour
ok?.......right.' He put the phone down and sat
thoughtfully for a moment. 'Well we have
underestimated Mister George North haven't we eh?'

Randall shifted uneasily. 'Underestimated how?'

Palmer took a deep breath. 'Our friend the Mayor
has had the MDs of all three major mobile phone
networks on the line to him. Each one has had a ten
million pound ransom demand and each has been told
to refer to the Mayor's office for details.'

The Mayor's office was very quiet. Palmer finished
explaining the situation to the three astonished mobile
phone network MDs and sat back. 'So you see
gentlemen, he can do what he says, he's proved that.
And by doing it he not only kills roughly a quarter of
a million innocent customers of yours but, as I am
sure you have already realised, puts you out of
business.'

The Mayor frowned. 'How?'

Palmer eyed him seriously. 'Have you answered a
mobile phone call since the other day?'

'Not likely!'

'Exactly and nor will anybody else once this whole
thing goes public. Nobody will want to know about
mobile phones let alone use them.'

'We'd be finished overnight.' The Celcall MD stated
the obvious.

'Pay him off, we have to pay him off.' Mr Premier
Network was getting very worried.

'And then what? He'll still have the means to do it?' Mr Global Transmitters was near to panic.

Sergeant Singh had been watching. She caught Palmer's eye. 'May I say something Sir?'

'Of course, go ahead.'

Singh looked from one to another of the MDs. 'How easy is it to close your networks down, and by that I mean keep the mast transmitters live but block any calls from coming into them?'

Silence greeted this for a moment.

'Close down?' Mr Celcall saw his company's revenue stream stopped in its tracks. 'Why close it down, North will just wait until we start up again and then do it?'

Singh smiled, 'Okay, just let me run this past you. Let's say North says he's going to make the calls at midday, so, at eleven fifty nine, by which time he's got his little box of tricks in position and ready, you shut the incoming call circuits down. He won't know the circuits are dead and when he makes his call he will be the only person making a call in the London area. His UHF transmitter has to be powerful enough for us to be able to pick him up on cross positioned scanners and pinpoint him by marking his signal from two different positions.'

'It could work the theory is sound.' Mr Top Phone was impressed.

Palmer saw a plan forming. 'So can you gentlemen arrange for a total shut down of your incoming call systems without it going public in advance? We need mister North out there with his signal so we can nab him.'

'If we want a business left afterwards we have to Chief Inspector.' The Celcall MD was still counting beans.

Palmer nodded. 'It's Chief Superintendent, good, then my Sergeant will be your contact point. When she says 'cut' you cut.'

Gheeta smiled benevolently at the three MDs. She addressed the Global Transmitters MD. 'I need a meeting with your server engineers as our man is on your network. I've an idea that may be of use but I need to work it through. Can we arrange that?'

'Of course, anytime you like.' Global Transmitters MD was grabbing at any straw.

Chapter 12

George North looked down from his sixth floor hotel room window onto London's busy Park Lane traffic. A smile of self appreciation crossed his face. Forty million pounds, a nice thought that, a very nice thought indeed. He checked the BBC News Channel on the hotel TV and then MSN news on his laptop. Still nothing in their bulletins about the Mayor being killed. North would have loved to have been there when he took the call on his mobile. Probably the police had put an embargo on the story. Can't frighten the population by telling them their Mayor had been murdered by a phone call. He laughed out loud. Forty million, yes a very, very nice thought. He picked up his passport from the bedside table. Ahfed Garranchi, Diplomatic Attaché, Italian Embassy, Peru. Amazing what money can buy.

Two floors above him on the hotel roof a mobile phone mast stood grey against the sky buzzing softly as it facilitated ten thousand calls every second. In four days time if no money was paid it would become a Weapon of Mass Destruction.

Chapter 13

'It looks like it's got the measles.' Palmer stood in the team room with Randall looking at a map Sergeant Singh had spread out on a table. It was of London's mobile phone masts and she had inked the M25 in green as a border and within that circle was a mass of red dots, each one being a telecoms mast.

'I hope all those signals in the air really can't have an effect on the human brain guv. What with radio and telecoms and satellites and the rest of the signals buzzing around out there, think of all that going through your head every second of the day!'

Palmer smiled. 'Yes, and you still can't find a program worth watching on a Friday night can you eh?'

Randall leaned over the map. 'So where do we start, needle in a haystack is an understatement looking at this lot.'

'You two start with this.' Palmer picked up a spiral bound engineer's reference book and handed it to Randall. 'This is a full list of all the aerials and where they are. See if we can discount any because of their position or access. For instance, if an engineer needs a forty foot ladder or hoists to get up to the mast cross it off the list. It won't get rid of many but any that we can find to whittle the number down is a bonus, possibles and probables. North will have sorted his mast out by now and it's going to be one with easy access and a reasonably secure location where he can do his work unnoticed. Chop chop then, let's go, get on with it.'

'Guv take a peep at this. 'Palmer had forgotten about Claire working away at her keyboard in the corner. She turned in her chair and smiled excitedly. 'I think I've got an address for Mister North.'

Palmer crossed quickly at that remark and pulled a chair up beside her. 'Go on.'

'Well just routine really. I input George North into the Land Registry data base.'

'The what Registry?'

'Land Registry. It's a national database where the owners of every bit of land and property in the UK are listed. If you buy or sell a house your solicitor has to check with them to make sure you own it and then update the files to the new owner's name.'

'Right.'

'Anyway…there's loads of George Norths as you might imagine.'

'Is it legal for you to access the Land Registry database?' Palmer wasn't unduly worried whether it was or was not. He was just curious. He knew there were many databases that Sergeant Singh had hacked into and set up secret lines of communication with that were classified and password protected. Or so their owners thought. Banks, Building Societies and credit card companies for a start. She'd won a bet with him by having his credit card details and spending record for the past year up on a screen within three minutes. He turned to face Singh who had heard the question.

She smiled and nodded. 'That one is perfectly legal sir.'

'Okay Claire go on.'

'Well, checking with North's employment record he has lived in a company provided house or apartment for the past 16 years so I shifted the search down to the time prior to that. Another point is that he's a bachelor boy, most owners are husband and wife, so I restricted the search further to a single name owner.......there were still quite a few George Norths though.....so what about middle names........he hasn't got one, bit unusual but got the list down to just 16.'She pressed a key and the printer whirred. 'And hey presto there they are.' She whipped the printed sheet off and handed it to Palmer.

He beamed at it like a kid in a sweetshop with ten pounds to spend. 'That is good, well done Claire. Right then, let's get these out to the local boys and see what we can find.'

Three o-clock in the morning parked in a West Norwood side street was not Palmer's idea of Heaven, and it was drizzling. He sat in the back of the plain squad car with the local CID chief and a driver in the front. They all looked through the windscreen to a semi detached house fifty yards up the road.

'I bet he's not in.' Palmer was tired.

'I'd go with you on that Justin,' Inspector Mann of South Thames Division CID agreed, 'No movement in or out all evening and no lights going on or off. Bloody place is empty.'

The offside car door opened and Sergeant Singh slipped quietly in and smiled at Palmer.

'Good morning Sergeant, sleep well?' Palmer was being sarcastic. Singh and Randall had been here as long as he had.

Claire's print out had borne fruit with five addresses that couldn't be discounted from a suspect list due to lack of information on the 'George Norths' that lived at them. Four had proved to be totally innocent homes of somewhat bemused gentlemen all called George North for whom a visit from the local police had proved to be a novelty and just a little unnerving, especially being the plain clothes branch. The West Norwood one had proved more interesting. Preliminary enquiries by the local CID had turned up the fact that this George North had asked for no mail deliveries and elected to pick up his mail from a post office box instead. He was a very low profile person and a police officer posing as a gas fitter come to service the boiler had got no answer and on knocking at the neighbours, which was the real reason for the visit, had been told that Mr North had only been see very occasionally and never passed the time of day or even acknowledged his neighbours should they be around.

Palmer reached for the car door handle, 'Right then let's go see what we can find.'

They left the car and were joined by Randall, two uniformed officers and two firearms officers fully armed. They silently approached the front door through the small paved front garden.

'Not a flower lover is he.' Palmer observed the concrete.

'I think it's called 'low maintenance' these days guv,' said Sergeant Singh.

Palmer stopped Inspector Mann's hand just as he was about to push the front door bell.

'I'd rather he didn't know we are here Geoff, rather take him by surprise. And it's odds on he's not going to be in there anyway.'

Randall lent forward and whispered to Palmer. 'I'll go round the back Sir in case he does a runner that way.'

He nodded to Randall and gave him a minute to get round the back before indicating to the uniform officer to be ready to use the hand held door ram.

Inspector Geoff Mann smiled, he had worked with Palmer before and was used to his circumvention of the rules when it suited.

'Left the warrant in the car have you Justin?' He smiled a weary smile.

Palmer felt his pockets hurriedly. A feigned look of shook crossed his face. 'Do you know Harry I believe I have…..oh well, get it later eh?' He nodded for the door ram to be used.

1930's wooden doors don't take a lot of smashing to open them. One swipe with a ram on the lock was enough. The wood splintered around it and the door swung invitingly open.

'Careful!' Palmer held back Gheeta who was about to rush inside, 'This guy's clever, could be booby traps, after you gentlemen.'

The firearms officers entered slowly, weapons at the ready.

Chapter 14

George North lay on top of the hotel bed. A pay-per-view video flickered on the television but his attention was taken from it as one of the two mobile phones on the duvet beside him vibrated. He turned it off and keyed in a number on the second mobile phone into which he pushed a single jack plug that had its other end connected into a small eight inch cube black box. He pressed the call button and listened as the mobile rang out the number. The unmistakeable sounds of a mobile ringing tone came from the small speaker on the side of the cube.

'Come along mister Plod…answer the phone.'

Chapter 15

'Don't answer that unless you want to die!' Palmer
barked out the order when the mobile rang. They all
looked round at the small Nokia 140 lying on a side
table in George North's hall ringing invitingly. Its
aerial flashing like a tasty bait. He turned to Sergeant
Singh. 'Can we get a trace on that call when it ends?'

Singh shook her head. 'I can take the Sim card out
and get the number but trying to trace it will probably
just lead us through another mouse trap of proxy
servers Sir.'

'He knows we are bloody well *here*.' Palmer was
realising North was a very worthy adversary. 'He's a
clever one isn't he, leading us around and second
guessing our movements. Okay, get forensics in asap
and see if they can find anything in the house that
could tell us where he is. The bugger knew we were
here.'

'He could just be watching from up the road Sir.'
Gheeta thought that was the most likely way North
would know when the police were in the house and
when to make the call.

Palmer nodded negatively. 'No too simple for him.
No, he's a 'planner' he's got this whole caper planned
out to lead us through the hoops, give us little morsels
that lead us along and point us in different directions
so that he knows exactly what we are doing. We need
to upset the plan somehow so he panics and breaks
cover.' He stifled a yawn and checked his watch.
'Blimey is that the time! Come on leave forensics to
do their work. Let's go and get some sleep.'

Palmer got dropped off at home by a squad car as dawn was breaking over Dulwich and walked slowly up his front garden path admiring the flowers and their scent which always seemed stronger to him in the early morning air. Mrs P looked after the gardens, front and back and it was her passion. Manicured lawns and flower beds planted to give the optimum colour and fragrance all year round. She'd planted a new rose bed in the front garden earlier in the year and it was a feast of colour and perfume. He stood on tiptoe to smell a white rose called Peace covering the top of the fence between his house and his next door neighbour Mr Bejamin, known to everybody in the neighbourhood as Benji.

Benji was not one of Palmer's favourite people. An ex Advertising Executive in his early sixties with a liking for designer clothes, jewellery, fake tans and *'poncing around like a prat'* as Palmer put it. A new car every year and three expensive holidays, usually 'singles' cruises, to some far flung exotic island group. For some reason that Palmer couldn't understand Mrs P and her lady friends in the WI and Gardening Club thought Benji wonderful. Bald on top with a pony tail was the icing on the cake as far as Palmer was concerned. He'd said to Mrs P... *'you know what you find under every pony tail don't you eh?......an arsehole.'* She didn't appreciate that and had told him to wash his mouth out. Although the daughter of a petty South London criminal Mrs P had tried to pull herself and Palmer up the social ladder. In Palmer's case it was snakes and ladders...up one rung and down three. She long ago accepted that she wouldn't ever change him. In her deepest heart she didn't really want to. A rough diamond he was and a rough diamond he would always be. She was proud of his career, proud of the way they'd brought up their children and very proud of her house and gardens. It was all a million miles from the small terraced house in Milkwood Road, Loughborough Junction she and her three brothers had been brought up in. The garden there was a twelve foot square of cracked concrete that was usually piled high with very dubious merchandise her dad had 'found' and a ladder was always propped up against the back wall in case there was a knock on the door early in the morning and dad had to make a quick exit over the railway marshalling yard behind. The knock on the door and the quick exit was usually when the young DC Palmer came with a warrant. Something between them had clicked and the rest is history. Forty years on and both continued to surprise the other.

Palmer took another long sniff of the rose. The rose bed perfume was exquisite but through the leaves over the fence what Palmer saw was not.

'What the....? Ouch!' He pricked his hand as he pushed the rose apart for a better look. What he had seen was that a rather over large hot tub had been installed on Benji's front decking and was gently steaming away. Palmer pulled an iron chair from Mrs P's front lawn set of four and table and stood on it for a better view. It was indeed a very large hot tub. But then Benji would have to have the biggest and most expensive available or it wouldn't be Benji.

'It's bigger than your kitchen.' Palmer had come inside, patted the dog, washed and donned his pyjamas in the en-suite bathroom before going into the bedroom. Mrs P stirred as he took an aerial look out of the window at the hot tub.

'What time is it Justin?'

'Quarter past five. Have you see that hot tub Benji's had installed? Talk about big you could book a cruise in the bloody thing!'

Mrs P's voice was muffled from under the duvet as she tried to shield her face from the light thrown into the bedroom by Palmer opening curtain wider to look down at the tub. 'It's very nice Justin. He's invited thc Gardening Club round to Christen it next week.'

'What? I hope you are kidding. Are they going to put their cozzies on and jump in?'

Mrs P's head appeared, her eyes blinking in the light. 'Of course we are. How else would you christen a hot tub? I'm looking forward to it. Champagne and buffet all provided by Benji.'

'You're going?'

'Yes and you're invited as well.'

'No way, too dodgy that. Some of those Garden Club members are a bit old.'

'So?'

'Well…… just thinking about incontinence that's all.'

'Don't be so vulgar Justin. Trust you to think of that.'

'And flatulence. Knowing Benji he'll have lots of those silly little floating perfume candles. If you see any bubbles coming up extinguish all naked flames!' He laughed. He was enjoying the thought of the Gardening Club members in a hot tub. 'And there's Benji's fake tan too. That might wash off and you'll all get out with a beige tint!' He laughed even more.

Mrs P swung her legs out of bed and stretched. 'Well, thank you for waking me so early,' She said sarcastically. 'I might as well get up now. Do you want anything to eat?'

'No, I'm going to catch a couple of hours sleep and then grab a bar of soap and have a bath in his tub when he's out. Save on our heating won't it eh? I take the dog in with me.' He was still giggling.

She gave him a withering look. 'If anything happens to that hot tub Justin Palmer, you will be first name in the frame.'

Chapter 16

Palmer exhaled loudly. He was in a small café off Trafalgar Square sitting opposite Commander Layne. He took a sip from his coffee and cleared his throat.

'Thank you Harry. Not what I wanted to hear but I appreciate you keeping me in the loop.'

The Commander shrugged. 'Least I could do Justin. But you didn't hear it from me okay? It really is one of those *for your eyes only* things. Upstairs wanted to let it roll on but I could see trouble ahead with that strategy.'

Chapter 17

North's mobile was humming on the hotel bed. He picked it up. 'Yes.'

The voice on the other end was curt, 'You got the Mayor's secretary, not the Mayor.'

'Damn! I wondered why there wasn't anything on the News about it.'

'We need a high profile victim George. They won't pay up no matter how many Joe Publics you kill but one celebrity and the cheque will be in the post right away.'

'Any suggestions?'

'No, but I was thinking. You're in a top hotel. They must get 'names' staying there. Easy to ring their room number and ……' the voice trailed off.

'Of course,' North smiled. 'Okay leave it with me.'

The line clicked off. He crossed the room and looked out of the window down onto the small drop off and pick up point in front of the Hotel where a queue of five limos and taxis waited for their passengers or were dropping them off.

Chapter 18

'Who?' Palmer raised his eyes from reading George North's CV and looked across the office with an inquisitive expression.

'Jamie Donnello.' Gheeta felt an explanation was in order as she knew Palmer's knowledge of the entertainment world could at best be described as nil. 'He is, or he was,' she explained, 'the winner of a television talent show last year. He's just had a number one single and was on a national tour.'

'Jamie Donnello?' Palmer was none the wiser.

'Yes.'

'Sounds like Spanish for Jammy Dodger.' He rose from his desk and started to put on his jacket and trilby. 'I take it you're telling me that he's been found dead in his hotel room because of the circumstances of his death are similar to our other corpses?'

'Trickle of blood from the ear guv,' she said it in a resigned manner, shut her laptop and put it into its shoulder case and followed Palmer out of the office and down the stairs.

'Big name was he?'

'As big as they get these days guv. All over the teen magazines, signed a big money deal with a record company, plenty of TV exposure and a million and a half twitter followers.'

'Million and a half twits more like, and he'll be forgotten next year when the next one hit wonder comes along.'

'Yes guv.' Gheeta didn't bother to answer him although she was quite fond of Donnello's songs. She had long suffered Palmer's scathing remarks about

TV talent shows and a certain Simon Cowell's fortune made on the back of people's misplaced hopes.

They crossed the Foyer and got the duty officers to pull a panda car in to ferry them to the Hotel. Palmer relaxed in the back. Gheeta pulled out her mobile.

'I'd better give Mark Randall a call and he can meet us there if he's free.'

Palmer waved a hand sideways. 'No don't bother him yet. I saw Commander Layne yesterday and Randall's pursuing another line of enquiry for him. We'll see what's what at the hotel first. I bet we won't be able to keep the media out of this one though, not if the record company sees a few thousand 'sympathy' sales of this bloke's records on the horizon.'

Gheeta shock her head in mock disbelief. 'Guv, only you would think that way.'

He laughed. 'Yes, me and the record company Sergeant. Give the Yard's PR department a ring and see if we can put out a press release limiting the death to 'unknown causes'. Being a pop star the media will think straight away it's drug related and they'll be off trying to find links between Mister Dodger and his dealers. That should give us some time.'

'Donnello guv, Mister Donnello.'

'Didn't I say that?'

'You know you didn't guv.'

Palmer smiled, 'Have you got a hot tub Sergeant?'

Gheeta wondered where on earth the conversation was going now. What had a hot tub to do with Donnello's murder? 'I live on the fifth floor guv.'

'Mmmmm.' Palmer dropped the subject as they pulled up outside the very opulent Majestic Hotel, Park Lane. Palmer was impressed. 'I Don't think Donnello's royalties would go very far in this place.'

They left the police car and fought through a melee of press people helped by the sharp elbows of the commissionaire and Palmer's size elevens 'accidentally' tapping a few ankles on the way. Once inside the manager introduced himself and took them by lift to the 3rd floor and Donnello's suite. The West End Central CID was working inside with forensics. The local Detective Sergeant stepped forward as they entered.

'DS Lydbrook sir, West End Central.'

Palmer introduced Sergeant Singh and took a look at the body lying beside the bed. The telltale trail of blood from the right ear had dried in place looking like a narrow scar. He straightened up, 'Okay Sergeant, bring us up to date.'

Lydbrook cleared his throat as though about to deliver a long speech.

Palmer anticipated it. 'Short and concise please Sergeant if you would. Time is of the essence.'

'Well Sir, the Hotel Housemaid found the body when she came in to do the daily clean about ten this morning. Local doctor was called and pronounced the lad dead and called us in as he was suspicious about the blood from the ear and thought it might be drug related.'

'Really?' Palmer was surprised at that. 'I thought you shoved Charlie up your nose not in your ear?'

Gheeta had to turn away stifling a smile. She knew this was Palmer having a kick at present day Doctors, most of whom he felt the cash strapped NHS ferried in from India with fake diplomas to cover their shortcomings in training up local people.

Lydbrook thankfully ignored the remark and carried on. 'The room's clear, no weapons, no syringe, no pills, nothing. The local beat man called it in to the station which is when the front desk recognised it fitted your flyer about corpses with blood around the ear. And that's about where we are at sir.'

Gheeta was looking at the body from all angles. 'Where's his mobile? Has it been bagged?'

Lydbrook gave a negative nod of the head. 'No nothing's been touched or removed.'

'So he hasn't got one?'

'If he has we haven't found it yet.'

Palmer was following Gheeta's train of thought, no mobile so the death call must have come on the land line. He turned to the Manager. 'Did you put the phone receiver back on the hook?'

The manager was unaware of the significance of his answer, 'Of course it was hanging and buzzing.'

Palmer understood why he would have replaced it not being aware of the phone's part in the murderl. He motioned Gheeta to the window out of earshot of the others. 'We have two possible scenarios as I see it, either an outside call coming in or an in-house call from another hotel room. Could North kill with his machine by putting it through on an internal phone?'

Gheeta was sure. 'Yes it's the sound frequency that's the weapon and that can be delivered to the ear through the digital chip on any phone. They use the same chips for internal and external phones.'

Palmer was worried. 'Better get down to the hotel switchboard and see if the last call into this room was internal or from outside. If it was internal then North either came in and made it from a phone in the foyer or lounge or some other public area in the hotel or he's booked a room. He's upping the ante. He's twisting the Mayor's arm a bit harder by killing a 'name'. I bet he waited for a high profile victim to check in, probably by sitting in the foyer, noted their room number and bingo! He made the call.'

Gheeta nodded. 'I'll check it. And I'll check the hotel CCTV too if they've got one.' Her mobile rang. They looked at each other. 'I'm almost afraid to answer it.' The screen showed it was Claire calling. 'It's okay it's Claire.' She took the call. Palmer wandered back over to the manager who was visibly shocked.

'My Sergeant is going to check your phone records and see who rang mister Donnello from outside and inside the hotel,' he said and smiled one of his reassuring smiles at the manager. 'Don't worry it's just normal procedure. By the way how did the press get on this story so fast? We had to fight our way through them to get in.'

The manager replied in a shaky voice. 'Probably from one of our staff Superintendent I'm afraid we get a lot of celebrities staying here. To be honest I don't agree with it but the policy is to offer the big agencies a very good deal so we get their 'name' clients. It's good for business but the down side is that the tabloids and celebrity magazines will offer staff a good cash incentive to leak any tasty stories.'

'It's Chief Superintendent, what are tasty stories?'

'Oh sorry, you know the type. Who's visiting who and staying all night, that sort of thing.'

'Oh I see.' He noticed Sergeant Singh beckoning him back. 'Excuse me a moment.' He crossed over to her.

She spoke quietly. 'The Mayor's office has had another call. Donnello's name was given and the money has gone up a million with the threat of further big name victims to come if it isn't paid. The Mayor's got the jitters and wants to pay. And the Yard's press office are fielding calls from just about every media company in England about Donnello's 'mysterious' death and the rumours about a serial killer on the loose in London.'

'Oh shit!' Palmer took a big breath. 'It's North, he's breaking the story so the Mayor panics and pays.' Palmer thought for a few moments. 'I'll go and have a word with the Mayor we need him to stall for a while. I'll get him to give the impression he's going to pay up and that it will take a little time, red tape, treasury blocking it or some such excuse ….should give us some precious time.'

Gheeta nodded. 'I'll go and check the phone calls and CCTV. I think I'd better take the manager with me and get him a strong cup of tea he looks like he's about to collapse into a quivering wreck.'

Palmer cast a glance the manager's way, 'I think he's probably more worried that the only phone calls he's going to get are room cancellations. Can't see anybody wanting to book in here now can you? Tomorrows headlines should just about kill his business…Murder at the Majestic! Read all about it!'

Gheeta smiled. 'I'll see if the doctor's got a sedative I can slip in his tea.'

Chapter 19

'Peru?'

It was the next morning. The Serial Murder Squad team room was buzzing. Palmer's officers were sifting through anything they could find on North and going out in pairs to check it. It was a hard task as this man was a loner with a high security ID and was positioned a long way beneath the radar. But as usual 'JCB' Claire had managed to dig up one surprising fact for the team.

Palmer repeated. 'Peru? He's been to Peru four times in the last six months? Are you sure?'

Claire nodded. 'Positive'

Sergeant Singh entered with a hand full of papers and photos. They exchanged pleasantries.

'Claire reckons North has visited Peru a few times lately.'

'Has he?' Gheeta asked Claire.

'Four times.'

Palmer was inquisitive. 'How do you know?'

Claire threw a 'shall I tell him look' at Gheeta. Palmer understood that look.

'Oh I see,' he smiled, 'one of Sergeant Singh's little programmes eh?'

He was well aware that Singh had hacked into just about every data base and Government department back office system that the team could ever want to glean information from whether they had restricted access or not.

Gheeta explained. 'Border Control Main Frame data base Sir. It lists all UK incoming and outgoing people from their passport numbers. Government uses it to massage the immigration figures. What they do is......'

Palmer cut her short. 'I don't want to know. I take it we are not supposed to have access to it?'

Gheeta struck an over-the-top innocent expression. 'I couldn't possibly comment Sir.'

'Okay, carry on Claire. What have you got?'

Claire smiled at Gheeta and continued. 'North has flown out to Peru from four different UK airports which was a bit silly really because if he did that to try and hide the flights it had the opposite effect because it was his name making unusual detours to get to Peru that flagged him up. Each time he's been there just a few days and then come back.'

'Well,' Palmer raised his eyebrows. 'So that's where our serial killer is making his nest eh? Get Interpol in Peru to see if they can quietly see what he's been up to. I'll lay money that he's bought a place and set up a bank account in one of those 'ask no questions' banks. And put a 'person of interest' flag on his passport with Border Control. If he tries to leave the UK they are to detain him and notify us immediately.'

'There is one other thing Sir,' Claire was serious. 'He's got a flight booked from Heathrow next Thursday.'

'Oh Christ! So that means he thinks he's going to have the money wired out and everything settled by then.' Palmer rubbed his chin thoughtfully.

'Sir,' Gheeta was worried, 'if he's not paid off by then he's going to try the big kill.'

Palmer nodded. 'You bet he will and if he gets an idea that the Mayor is stalling he's likely, probably more than likely, to arrange more demonstrations of his little box's power.'

'We do have one glimmer of hope Sir.' She looked at one of the papers she was carrying. 'The call made to Donnello was an internal one from the Hotel lobby. It's not much but it's something.'

Palmer shrugged. 'So either North was staying there or came off the street to make the call? The only way he'd know Donnello's room number was if he overheard it at reception or followed him up to the room.'

'He followed him up in the lift.'

'How do you know?'

She passed a clutch of photo prints over to Palmer. 'Prints of stills taken off the hotel CCTV. They show North getting into the same lift as Donnello and his agent and getting out on the same floor and then walking a few yards behind the pair of them as they went to his room. He's then picked up on the foyer camera sitting reading a paper until the agent left and then he goes out of shot presumably to make the killer call.'

'I reckon he was staying there you know. I can't see the hotel staff not picking up on a bloke who's not a guest or resident wandering around, going up and down in the lift, sitting in the foyer,' Palmer was leafing through the stills, 'Security in a posh hotel like that would be all over him in no time.'

Gheeta took the stills back and put them into her shoulder bag. 'I'll get over there and show these around. See if anybody recognises him. It could be he's still there. That'd make our job easier wouldn't it eh?'

Palmer waved a finger at her. 'Well if he is don't do anything silly. Get back to me. I'm going to go see the Mayor again and keep him under control. Make sure he plays ball.'

The Mayor didn't want to play ball.

'Justin, I've had my secretary killed when it could easily have been me. Three of my constituents are dead and now a pop singer is dead and all for the sake of a few million quid. The media are onto it and if I don't pay up can you imagine what will happen if he did manage to kill a few thousand? Can you? Pandemonium Justin and one head on the block…mine.'

Palmer nodded sympathetically. 'I fully understand that mister Mayor. I'm not saying don't pay him. Although if you do, as I've said before, what's to stop him coming back for more at a later date?'

The Mayor laughed. 'I would have thought eleven million from me and ten million from each of the three networks would be enough to set him up for life wouldn't you? I can't see that he'd ever need to come back for more.'

'I'm just covering all the bases. Anyway I haven't said don't pay him. All I've said is to stall paying him for as long as you can. Believe me we are getting very close to him now and with the networks on board with their ability to be able to switch the power off we can neutralise his actions.'

'Only if you know when and where he's going to send that damn signal out. How will you know that eh?'

'I don't know that, not yet anyway. But I do know that as long as he thinks all that cash is coming his way fairly soon he won't jeopardise *that* pay day. Just stall him, tell him the Council's broke and you've got to arrange a loan from some Monetary Fund or the Bank of England. Tell him he must understand that you can't tell them what the money is for as Government policy is not to pay ransoms to terrorists, which is what he is after all, so you're finding it difficult.'

The Mayor let out a long sigh. 'Okay, but one more death because of the stalling Justin and I'll pay him.'

Chapter 20

Commander Layne was waiting outside a large solid steel rear gate on a narrow back lane into Gatwick Airport when Palmer's plain squad car pulled up. Palmer lowered his passenger side window as the Commander approached.

'Don't blame us if we are a bit late Harry. I never knew there were so many little lanes and tracks out here. We've been going up and down them like a ferret up a drain pipe. Sat Nav has stopped working which didn't help.'

'I know. That's us, we block out all communication signals around here except our own. No Sat.Nav. and your phone won't work either.' Commander Layne smiled and pointed to a dark car pulled up, lights off, further back along the lane. 'We wouldn't let you get lost Justin, we've been watching you.' He made a signal and the car moved past them and away. The gates swung open. 'Go through and park on the right by the hanger.'

Palmer's driver edged through the gates which closed behind them. Palmer noted civilian armed personnel either side in the shadows. His driver pulled the car to a halt beside a long unlit single story building. Layne opened Palmer's door. He had a military uniformed person with him.

'Justin you and I will go inside and my Corporal will take your driver for some refreshments.'

'I'm okay sir, got a flask with me thank you,' the driver explained.

Palmer lent towards him. 'I don't think that was an offer you can refuse. Better go with the Corporal.'

They left the car and Layne took Palmer through a side door into a very large open plan hanger. But instead of an aeroplane inside which he had expected to see the place was full of camouflaged tanks and two matt black unmarked helicopters. Layne was aware of Palmer's surprise.

'First law of warfare Justin, control the skies. And to control the skies you need control of the airport.'

'Are we at war?'

'No but being ready for war is the second law.' They walked around the perimeter of the floor space. 'We have one of these units at every strategic UK airport Justin all terribly 'hush-hush' but very useful.'

'Useful?'

'Can't render a hooded and shackled terrorist off to a friendly Arab State for questioning through the public departure lounge can we eh? If the Government needs to get somebody out on the quiet this is a very secure way of facilitating it.'

'Why you you're Navy not RAF?'

'N14 actually.'

'Say no more,' said Palmer, he knew any questions about N14 wouldn't get an answer. At the end of the hanger was a guarded lift door. The guard nodded to Layne as they entered the lift and Palmer noted it had four floor buttons and they were at the fourth floor. Down they went to floor two and when the door opened and they stepped out it was like entering a modern hotel reception area. The difference being that the staff wore military uniforms and a bank of CCTV screens filled one wall. Layne led Palmer past the desk and down a corridor of what Palmer took to be cell doors. At the end they entered a small viewing gallery and through the one-way glass could see Mark Randall sat at a table. Both wrists shackled to it and two guards standing behind him.

Layne pointed through the glass. 'He's not talking. That's the trouble. These chaps are trained to withstand rough interrogation and of course we can't go down that route. Geneva Convention and all that. No water-boarding allowed here.'

'I'm glad to hear it.'

Layne smiled. 'So we just fly them out to Saudi or Kuwait and do it there.'

'Do you sleep at night Harry?'

'I do, but I wouldn't if I didn't have units like this one watching out for us. Think of it that way.'

'I can see your point. Could you do it in a hot tub?'

Layne looked mystified. 'Do what, water-boarding?'

'Sorry, don't know why I said that. Right then where do we go from here with Mister Randall then I need to find North pretty quickly now? The Mayor's going to stall him but how long he'll keep that up and how long North will wait until he realises it's a stall and presses the button is anybody's guess.'

'Right, let me fill you in on mister Randall. As I told you in our private café meeting we cottoned onto Randall being in cahoots with North a few weeks ago and we know he's been feeding North information so that he keeps one step ahead of us. I decided to let Randall run with it but when you told me about the Peru thing I thought it best to bring him in as we don't want the pair of them fleeing with the money if it all goes wrong. No extradition treaty with Peru.'

'It won't all go wrong. What's the connection between Randall and North?'

'Randall was North's PO, protection officer, when North was working at Portman Down. People working on new WMDs are targets for other countries that try and get them to jump ship and bring their work with them. And that's not only enemy countries but friendly ones as well. America is the main culprit. Bit like the Premier League in football. A top scientist gets offered a financial package he can't refuse and gets tempted to move. So people like Randall are supposed to keep an eye on their marks and let us know if that is happening. Somewhere along the line this gamekeeper turned poacher and saw that North's ultra sound weapon was a WMD game changer of enormous value and assisted him in smuggling the parts out and then disappearing. Every time we got within touching distance of North he would be gone. It became pretty clear he was getting inside information and that pointed at Randall. When you lot became involved after the murders we decided to let you run with it in the hope that without Randall on your team keeping North up to speed you'd have a good chance of nailing him. Little did we know that Randall was shacked up with your Detective Sergeant and was privy to all your moves as well as ours!'

'I didn't know that either until you told me. I keep my squad's private life away from the office. How did you find that out?'

'I got MI6 to do a deep security check on Randall. Got a shock when it came back with that little bombshell I can tell you. So that's when I decided to have our little café meet and fill you in.'

Palmer thought for while. 'Yes, well I have to admit I tested your theory out when we did a raid on North's West Norwood house. The only way North could have known we were inside and to phone us at that particular time in the morning was if somebody let him know. And the only person who could have done that was Randall who suggested he go round the back of the house on his own just before we went in. He must have had a pre arranged signal that he sent to North. That personal relationship with Sergeant Singh gives me a lever I can use. Shall we get on with it?'

Layne led Palmer out of the viewing gallery, down a few stairs and into the interview room. Randall looked surprised to see Palmer who sat down opposite him whilst Layne stood away by the door.

'Bit of a bastard aren't you eh?' Palmer snapped at Randall who looked a bit shocked at the veracity of the attack. 'Making out you care for Gheeta. Moving in, taking all her true affections and giving back your false ones just to get information on North. You're a little shit Randall. You're not a man. Just a two faced little shit. She still loves you. Won't grass on you. Right now she's banged up in West End Central. She says she was not working with you but it's obvious you persuaded her to join you and North in your money making scheme. She denies it but it's obvious she's as guilty as you. She gave you the information on what was happening and you passed it to North. No wonder he's always a step ahead of us. Well sorry old son but neither you nor her are going to get the life of bliss in Peru you had lined up for yourselves, more likely to be Pentonville. A tiny cell in a maximum security wing locked up for twenty three hours a day. Twenty four if I had my way. You know, you remind me of the blokes who befriend vulnerable females and steal their life savings…..only you stole her heart and her career. CPS reckons the pair of you will go down for assisting murder and if North manages to do anymore it'll be mass murder. That's life in any Judges book Randall. Pity, DS Singh was a brilliant detective with a glittering career ahead of her. A family that loves her and then you came along and fucked it all up. Nice bloke aren't you eh?'

Randall spoke in a whisper. 'She's not involved.'

Palmer laughed. 'Bollocks! She's in it up to her neck.'

Randall looked up and spoke loudly. 'She's not. It was just a coincidence she was on the North case. She didn't even know what I did. She thought I was security consultant. She's nothing to do with it. I should have told her I was on the case but knowing your moves in advance was a Godsend.'

'Wasn't it just! But the only place it's going to send you old son is inside, forget Peru. I'll see if we can arrange the two of you have cells opposite so you can explain to her over the next thirty years or so what a bastard you are. Romantic really isn't it eh? You'll be able to grow old together……inside.'

Randall shouted with an angry voice. 'She's not fucking part of it you fool. She had nothing to do with it!' He was shaking at the shackles.

Palmer had him. He lent forward on the table and shouted into Randall's face, 'No of course not, nothing to do with it. Your living with a key member of the murder squad who is after your big mate who is about to share forty million quid with you and she's nothing to do with it? She's up to her neck in it. What was her share to be then, five million? Bit more than a Detective Sergeant earns I can tell you.' He turned away as if to leave, had second thoughts and returned to put his face into Randall's again. 'Okay mister lover boy…..you know that you are going down for a considerable time, you're not going to Peru or any other place with no extradition ties to the UK and you're not getting *one* pound let alone forty million of them, so if Sergeant Singh is as innocent as you say she is just tell me where North is and if we can get to him before his moment of madness I'll see that the court is told that you assisted us. That might just get the judge to reduce the sentence so you might get out with a few years of your miserable life left to enjoy in civvy street. And, when we do get North, if he knows nothing about Sergeant Singh I might be minded to believe she's as innocent as you say.' He stayed with his face barely twelve inches from Randall's for what, to Layne, seemed an eternity. Randall knew he was in a tunnel with no light at the end and Palmer had just lit a very small one.

His voice dropped to a whisper. 'She has nothing to do with it,' he paused for a moment. 'He's still in the hotel. He's going to wire into the telecoms mast on its roof.' His head dropped to the desk. 'Tell her I'm so sorry, tell her I love her.'

'No way,' said Palmer over his shoulder as he hurried out of the interview room and scuttled along the corridor with Layne trying to keep up. 'Find my driver Harry. My Sergeant has gone to that bloody hotel with North's mug shot and if the staff recognise him as a resident she might try and be a hero…..she should have more sense but who knows.'

Layne was confused, 'I thought you said she was in custody? In cahoots with Randall and North?'

'Did I say that Harry?' he smiled at Layne. 'Sometimes I am such a liar. Can't help it.'

Commander Layne despatched one of his men to fetch the driver from the visitor's refreshment room. 'You haven't lost your touch Justin have you eh? Brilliant strategy that! Mind you just one thing you got wrong.'

'And what's that?' They were in the lift going up to ground level.

'He's not going to Pentonville or any other civilian prison. It will be a closed military court martial and a military prison to follow probably on an overseas base like Malta. None of this will ever get out. Media would have a field day if they thought we'd let a mad scientist with a homemade WMD go AWOL.'

'Well let's hope we get him before he gets to use it then,' replied Palmer as they exited the lift and ran through the array of tanks and helicopters on the ground floor to the exit door. 'Mind you Harry, it is kind of comforting to know this is all here should we need it. Frightening and comforting at the same time.'

Outside they got to Palmer's car as his driver arrived. Palmer winced as he got in. 'Damn sciatica…shouldn't have run just now, gets me now and again. I'll keep you in the loop Harry.' They shook hands through the window.

Layne was very serious. 'Just remember when you get him he's our military prisoner. Let me know and

I'll have him picked up. I could go into that hotel with a team if you prefer Justin?'

  'Oh yes, and that would set the media alight wouldn't it eh?'

  'Just thought I'd offer, you take care old friend and give my best to Mrs P.'

Chapter 21

At the hotel Sergeant Singh was most surprised to find that North was immediately recognised by the Manager and that he was still in residence. Room eighty eight fourth floor. She tried unsuccessfully several times to get Palmer on his mobile and even through the control room channel at the Yard but he couldn't be raised. She decided that being in uniform she'd better keep out of sight just in case North came down from his room and got spooked by it. So she sat in the manager's office behind reception. A large one way glass window in the door gave her a good view of the foyer if North should leave. Her mobile rang. It was Palmer.

'Where are you?'

'At the hotel, North is still here guv.'

'Yes I know, don't go near him. There's a firearms unit on its way. Get a side room for them to use to tool up. I've told them to come in one by one looking like guests. They'll give my name at reception. Okay?'

'Bit like James Bond this isn't it guv? I'll arrange a room for them.'

'Okay Moneypenny,' he laughed, 'and get through to your network contacts and get the signals from that mast on the hotel roof cut off. That's the one he's going to use. He might have hot wired into it already so softly, softly is the word. If he gets an inkling we are onto him he might just press the button.'

'Okay I've been trying to contact you. You had your mobile turned off?'

'No. I got into a dead area. I'll fill you in later. I'm on my way. Oh and get a pass keycard off the manager so we can get into North's room.'

'Okay.'

She got a pass card and then had the manager label a side lounge as 'Private Meeting' and one by one eight firearms officers arrived, all in civilian clothes and all with the same large suitcase which Singh thought amusing. Reminded her of an old Pinewood comedy film with Peter Sellers that her dad used to watch and laugh at. They all gave their name as 'Palmer' and were directed by the Manager to the side lounge. Sergeant Singh waited until they were all present and then briefed them on the situation with North. All they wanted to know was where he was in the hotel, was he armed and was he wanted alive? She told them his room and floor, that he was probably armed, but she thought it best not to say armed with a WMD, and she gave them each a print out of his face taken from the lift interior CCTV. Then she rang the networks and had the signal from the roof mast switched off.

Palmer arrived as the evening became dark outside. 'Right lads I want to impress on you that this bloke is very dangerous. When and if you get him in view he is likely to try and make a call on a phone or click a switch or press a button on some sort of trigger apparatus. We've got that covered so let him do that but he must not be allowed to get away. Understand?'

A chorus of grunts acknowledged the command. Palmer handed the logistics of the operation over to the SFO, Senior Firearms Officer who sent three through the kitchens and up the staff staircase to the fourth floor where North's room was. Two more went up the main guest staircase where the hotel put a 'Cleaning in Progress' sign at the bottom and diverted all guests to the lifts, and another two stayed covering the ground floor and lifts out of view in the Manager's office. Palmer and Gheeta took the lift up with the last one.

Chapter 22

North was getting impatient. He checked his watch. Quarter past four. Randall should have been in touch by now with an update on the police activity. He guessed the Mayor was probably playing for time on police orders. He should have been out of the country on his way to a very wealthy life in Peru by now if things had gone to plan. The fly in the ointment was the Mayor. Time to call him one last time and then if the money wasn't wired out it would be time to show just what he could do. He was angry. He picked up one of the two mobiles on the hotel telephone table, clipped a voice distorter over the mouthpiece and pressed the Mayor's direct number on speed dial. It rang five times, enough time for the trace equipment in the Mayor's office and the operators to start a trace. North smiled. He'd covered all that by using Eastern European proxy servers and knew the trace would go round and round in circles. The Mayor answered.

'Hello.'

'Where's my money?'

'It's all in hand.'

'It's not in my hands. You have thirty minutes to have it wired out to the account I gave you. Thirty minutes.'

'It's the Treasury they're taking time to put it together. You can't just wire ten million without official sanction. It will be there. Just give me a bit more time.'

'Thirty minutes and it's now eleven million. If it's not done in thirty minutes say goodbye to a million voters. Your choice. Thirty minutes.' He clicked off. Time to prove he was not a man to be messed with. The M.O.D. should have realised that when they cut his funding and shelved his project. They thought he was bluffing. Well now they would find out that he wasn't. He took a suitcase from the wardrobe and delved down to bottom where his small box of death was hidden. Picking up the two mobiles and putting them and his little box into his jacket pockets he checked the corridor through the spy hole, all clear. Leaving the room quietly he hung the 'Do Not Disturb' sign on the door and made his way along to the end of the corridor and quickly through the staff door onto the staff staircase. It wasn't clear. He could hear people coming up from below. Slowly he peered over the rail and down. Hotel staff don't usually wear all blue flack jackets and carry Heckler and Koch MP5SF sub machine guns. The two men two floors down and on their way up did. North quickly drew back out of sight. His brain raced. He'd obviously been found. But how, Randall? Must be Randall, he hadn't checked in when he should have. He must have been found out somehow. Perhaps Randall talked to save his own skin otherwise how would the police know he was here? Five minutes more in the hotel room and he'd probably have been caught. North knew he was now on his own. He kept tight against the staircase wall and went up the flights silently. On the top floor, the seventh, he stopped and listened. No sound from below. A careful look down showed no activity. Whoever that was coming up, and he guessed it was either a police firearms unit or SAS, had left the staircase. Probably left it at his floor to burst into his room. He pushed open the door to the roof. The cool air and sound of London's traffic hit him. How long had he got? The game was obviously up. He wasn't going to get the money and he probably wasn't going to get away. Okay Mister Mayor let's see how you explain away the deaths of a few thousand of your electors for the sake of a few million pounds then eh? See how you like being cast on the scrap heap like I was. In front of him bolted securely to the top of the water tower stood the sturdy thirty foot steel telecommunications gantry looking like something from War of the Worlds awaiting an order to rip itself from the restraining bolts and attack. The light from tall office buildings around the hotel reflecting from it made it stand out against the dark red sky above. The three major network satellite dishes stood out proud from the sides amongst a host of other smaller discs and antennae. North smiled, okay mister Mayor, okay MOD let's see who has the last laugh. He started to climb the steel rungs of the water tower ladder.

The lift doors opened on the fourth floor and the firearms office furtively looked out and checked the corridor. At either end his men from the staff staircase knelt on one knee their weapons ready. He signalled to them and they advanced along the corridor hugging the walls towards room 88. Palmer and Gheeta followed behind. At the room an officer checked through the spy hole. No movement inside. Gheeta gave him the pass keycard which he silently slipped into the door card reader. He nodded to the other officers and with a substantial amount of noise they slammed open the door and rushed in shouting 'Police!!'

The rooms were checked, the cupboards and drawers were checked, the bed mattress was checked. Nobody, and nothing to say the room had even been occupied, the only clue was a used tea cup.

'Where the Hell is he then?' Palmer had a sinking feeling. If North had managed to get out of the Hotel he could be anywhere. And there was no way of getting to him until he made contact. And he might well make contact by using his box of tricks.

'Well we know he didn't go down Sir so he must have gone up.' Gheeta made the obvious observation.

They took three armed officers with them and followed in North's footsteps up the service stairs to the roof door. The officers went through quietly and signalled the all clear for Palmer and Gheeta to follow. Once through onto the roof they waited, crouched in the shadows against the wall as two officers searched around the roof checking behind the large air control fan units. They gave the all clear.

Palmer felt a tap on his shoulder. It was Gheeta's hand. He followed the direction her finger pointed. Upwards to the mast gantry above the water tower where the dark figure of North was crouching tight against the base.

'Mister North,' shouted Palmer, 'this is Chief Superintendent Palmer of the Metropolitan Police. Would you come down Sir please.' There was no reply. He tried again louder. 'Mister North we've had the phone signals cut off from this mast. Your weapon won't work. The game is over.'

After a short silence North shouted back. 'Do you think isolating this mast will make any difference Chief Superintendent? There are a hundred of these masts in London and my signal has the strength to reach quite a few of them from here. You'd better call the Mayor Chief Superintendent. I want to walk out of here and I want my money. Call him. He's five minutes left.'

Palmer looked at Gheeta. 'Is that right can his signal reach the other masts?'

'Depends on his power source guv. If the battery in his box is big enough....yes.'

'He's played his trump card then hasn't he but he's also signed his own death warrant.' He turned to the SFO in charge. 'Use the same procedure as for a terrorist with a suicide belt, aim for the head. He's got to go out like a light. Wait for my signal. I'll give a nod. I'm going over to try and distract him. When I see he's not got his finger on the box I'll give the nod and you take him out okay?'

The firearms officer nodded and aimed his weapon. Palmer stood ready to walk over to the base of the water tower.

Gheeta caught his arm and whispered. 'I have an idea guv, I talked it through with the engineer at Global technologies which is North's mobile network. Keep him talking as long as you can.' She pressed in a number on her phone and turned out of earshot.

Palmer responded to her request. 'You're not getting any money mister North and you've two choices of getting out of here. Come down now and walk out in handcuffs or try and use your little box of tricks and go out in a body bag. There are three sniper rifles trained on you right now.'

'Do you think that worries me Superintendent? Do you really? If I go then an awful lot of people go with me.' He held up his box of death. 'I've wired this into the networks and one little press on the switch and thousands of people will answer their phones and die. The networks don't discriminate between people Superintendent. Could be quite a lot of the rich and powerful in amongst that lot, MPs, Royalty, even maybe members of your own family. Think of that eh? Call the Mayor. He only has three minutes now.'

Palmer was unsure what to do. If the signal was going to be picked up through other masts then there was nothing he could do. People would die.

'It's *Chief* Superintendent and I've got the Mayor on the phone right now, he's doing his best.' Was all he could think to shout back. 'Where is the money to be wired to?'

North was getting angry. 'Stop playing games with me *Chief* Superintendent. The Mayor has all the details. You're just stalling me.'

Gheeta moved close and whispered urgently into Palmer's ear. 'One more call guv, for God's sake don't let him press the button yet.'

Palmer had no idea what she was doing as she keyed in another number and turned to be out of sight and earshot of North but he knew he could trust her one hundred percent to know what she was doing. 'Where's your mate Randall then?' Palmer didn't want to bring Randall up now but couldn't think of another way of further stalling North. He noticed Sergeant Singh turn her attention to what he'd just said and then turn back again to continue on the mobile.

North was silent for a moment. So Randall was still around. The police hadn't got him. Then why hadn't he made contact where was he when he was needed?

'Two minutes Chief Superintendent, two minutes to Armageddon.'

The firearms officer leant in close to Palmer. 'Shall we take him out sir?'

Palmer thought quickly. 'No, I can't risk him pressing that button, can't risk him falling on it if you kill him. I'm going over to try and talk to him and try to get him to release the box from his hand, as soon as he does then take him.' He stood up. 'Mister North I'm coming over to talk.'

North laughed. 'Oh no Chief Superintendent I'm not having any of your funny business thank you. If you come within ten yards of me I press the button. One minute left.'

Gheeta whispered urgently into Palmer's ear. 'Every mast within forty miles is switched off, his machine is useless now.'

'What?' Palmer was incredulous. 'Are you sure?'

'Yes guv, no phone in the Greater London area will get his death call except one.'

'One, which one?'

'The Mayor's. It means North's box will show a green light and he will think all his signals have got through when they haven't. The Mayor won't be answering I've just spoken to him so don't panic guv. And then North will get a shock.'

Palmer looked into Sergeant Singh's eyes. 'Is this one of your technical jigsaws that you've got lined up?'

'Yes.'

'Are you sure it will work there are a lot of people's lives at risk here?'

'It will work guv, trust me'

'I always do Sergeant, okay.' He turned to the firearms officers, 'Go get him lads. No shooting he can't hurt you now.' He shouted to North. 'Mister North we are coming to arrest you now. Your plan has failed.'

North stood up out of the shadows and held his death machine in front of him for all to see. He could see the Officers coming for him. 'All right Chief Superintendent, if you and the Mayor want it to end this way so be it.' Theatrically he pressed a button on the machine. His mobile rang. He laughed loudly as he saw the screen indicate it was the Mayor's number. 'Oh my, the Mayor is calling me, I hope he's not ringing to say he's paid the money. Look a bit of a fool now won't he with a few million of his electorate dead.' He pressed the answer button and put the phone to his ear. 'Hello Mister Mayor.'

It seemed to Palmer that everything then went into slow motion. North's startled expression lasted for what seemed an eternity as the phone slid from his hand and he dropped to his knees. The wires tied into the mast pulled his box from his hand as he dropped and it swung on the end of them like a pendulum clattering against the steel mast with each swing. North's body slid slowly off the mast base onto the water tower where it rolled to the edge and fell the twenty foot to the hotel roof landing with a dull thud.

The firearms officers stood with their weapons pointing at the lifeless body as Palmer knelt and turned the head sideways. The line of blood from his ear was still shining in the reflected street light. He turned and looked up at Sergeant Singh.

'Just how did you manage that?'

She smiled. 'Simple I put 'call divert' on the Mayor's phone to North's phone.'

Chapter 23

The late night revellers of central London crowded round the Hotel entrance as North did indeed leave the hotel in a body bag as Palmer had warned him he would do. In the side lounge Palmer and Singh sat drinking very welcome cups of tea as the firearms team packed away their uniforms and weapons and left.

'So Sergeant,' Palmer moved into a comfortable arm chair, 'Tell me why I shouldn't charge you with murder? You didn't have to use the call diversion from the Mayor's phone. The signals were all cut off.'

'They were and if his box had registered that his signal wasn't getting through to any mobiles he may well have had an override capacity built in or even been able to input a repeat function into the networks computers so that when they turned the signal back on bingo! it went again. I couldn't take that chance guv. He was a very clever man top man in his field. But if even just one signal got through to just one phone it would register as okay on his box and he'd think it had worked. But that phone would have to be answered by somebody and who better than North himself? We knew his mobile number from his calls to our three victims and the Mayor's office.'

Palmer thought for a moment or two. 'If the Assistant Commissioner or PCC want answers I think it might be better to say that North's little box must have malfunctioned.'

Singh smiled. 'Okay Sir. Now, I want you to fill me in on Mark Randall's part in all this? I'm a bit confused.'

'Alright but you won't like it. Come on let's get a squad car and I'll drop you off at home and tell you the whole story on the way.'

Palmer got out of the squad car in front of his house, thanked the driver and breathed in the cool late night air. Detective Sergeant Singh hadn't seemed too upset by the subterfuge and double dealing of her now ex partner. He was pleased about that as Palmer wasn't one for extending a comforting arm or a shoulder to cry on. Mrs P had often told him he was devoid of emotions but the truth be known, he wasn't, he was just very good at hiding them. A skill developed over many years of police work.

He walked slowly up the drive as the scent from her roses wafted over him. He stood admiring the blooms and stepped into the bed leaning to smell a few individually. At the same time wondering why his feet felt wet, and looking down he saw that his shoes had sunk into the soft earth that was Mrs P's prize rose bed that was now drowned in a river of water coming under the fence from Benji's garden. On tip toe Palmer peered over the fence half knowing what he was going to see, and he wasn't wrong. A half empty luxury Hot Tub with a broken side panel was leaking gallons of water across the lawn and under the fence. The wonderful Benji would be getting an earful of Mrs P's anger in the morning. Palmer smiled, looked up towards the Heavens and mouthed the words 'thank you'. It had been a good day. And now it had just got better.

END

BOOK FOUR   **POETIC JUSTICE**

Chapter 1

Madame Geneelia did not look very nice dead. In fact she looked hideous. Death has a habit of stripping away the body cosmetic, the personality it once housed and leaving on view the basic flesh and shape helpless in its inadequacy to convey to the viewer even the slightest hint of the person it once housed. The person whose body it once belonged to has gone and now like an empty discarded pupa it is left behind, the empty host to an expired life.

  Madame Geneelia's body minus Madame Geneelia was quite a shock to Detective Chief Superintendent Justin Palmer head of Scotland Yard's Serial Murder Squad and his number two Detective Sergeant Gheeta Singh as they took their first look at it lying exposed on the hotel room floor. Madame Geneelia had obviously been dressed in only a bathrobe when she had opened her hotel room door to the killer who's vicious attack had sent her sprawling backwards onto the plush carpet where he or she had then repeatedly plunged a serrated steak knife into her ample chest which had presented itself as a suitable target when the robe had opened with the fall.

Chapter 2

The case had started for Palmer nine days before.
London had been wet that day. It was a Wednesday in
late May. Drenched commuters bent against the fierce
straight rain slicing down like water javelins from the
Heavens above Park Lane. They sought shelter in
already crowded shop doorways which provided short
lived remission from the wet onslaught as they waited
for their bus home. Folded soggy newspapers held
above their heads were a poor deterrent against the
aqua attack as their squinting eyes tried to pick out
the bus numbers through the spray which bounced off
the crawling traffic producing an ethereal wet mist.
  Palmer rocked slowly to and fro on his heels as he
looked down onto the scene from behind the thick
safety glass that served as a front wall to the second
floor Guest Lounge of the Majestic Hotel, Park Lane.
He sipped coffee from a hotel issue white stoneware
cup emblazoned with the hotel's elaborate crest
which he'd tried to decipher through boredom but
couldn't make head or tail of. He had elected to wrap
his hand around the cup and hold it like a mug after
several unsuccessful attempts to get a finger through
the ridiculously small aperture of the handle. The
coffee was good and he liked good coffee. It
reminded him of his days as a young Constable at
West End Central Police Station when a mug of good
hot coffee at the Lyon's Corner House in the Strand
would fortify him for the rest of his beat. Get four of
these piddling little hotel cups in one of those mugs
he thought to himself. A fresh squall of rain sent

rivers of water zigzagging down the outside of the glass wall making it hard to define anything outside. He turned to where his number two, Sergeant Gheeta Singh, in her regulation Metropolitan Police issue blue trouser suit, sat forward on a leather buttoned sofa beside a glass coffee table sipping her coffee. He noted she could get a finger through the blasted handle. She was flicking through a shiny fashion magazine. One of many that littered the coffee tables in the lounge. All offering overpriced 'designer' fashion garments mostly made for a few rupees in an Indian sweat shop. Palmer remembered an argument he'd had a while ago with Mrs P. about the power of advertising and how he reckoned that if he set up a ladies fashion range called *'Shite'* and advertised it enough in the glossy magazines and paid a third rate celebrity to wear it, it would be a success. He smiled recalling her reaction of feigned shock at his use of such a word and promising him that should he mention such an idea in front of her lady friends he would most certainly be in the *'shite'* himself!

He put his cup on the table and lowered himself into a plush, soft armchair that immediately enveloped him lovingly like an attacking giant marshmallow. There was something about luxury that wasn't to his liking. It pervaded you, dulled your senses. It didn't have any sharp edges. Or perhaps it was just that he couldn't afford it.

He exhaled loudly. 'Third week of May Sergeant and we're still getting April showers. Or April storms more like. Do you realise Sergeant it's the second week of British Summertime this week and all we've had is rain, rain and more rain.' He tried to reach forward for his coffee but the chair had got him trapped in its soft grip and wouldn't let go. 'I'll need a ruddy crane to get out of this chair.' Sergeant Singh passed him his coffee. He took a sip and relaxed back. 'Typical Wednesday this is, wet. Funny how you associate things with days isn't it?'

'Do you guv I hadn't really noticed?' The answer was automatic. She turned a page engrossed in an article on e-commerce fraud.

Palmer continued, 'Yes, Wednesdays is always wet. Mondays is 'here we go again another working week'......Fridays are 'hoorah weekend is here'......Saturdays is football day, well it used to be when I was a boy now every blooming day is football day, Tuesdays and Thursdays are blanks and Sunday is peace and quite good old Sunday eh?'

'Not where I live it isn't peace and quiet guv,' She shot him a glance before returning to the article.

'Well,' he shifted his backside which the chair was gradually devouring within its soft cushions, 'If you choose to live in the middle of a Leisure Centre then you must expect Joe public to use it at the weekend for his leisure....this damn chair is swallowing me!'

'The Barbican isn't a Leisure Centre guv.'

Palmer struggled up a little. 'Oh no? If the Thames flood gates fail it'll be a ruddy aquarium never mind a leisure centre.' He chuckled to himself as he sank further into the chair, 'I'll need a lifebelt in a minute. I could get very used to this comfortable style of living.'

'Not on Police pay you couldn't guv.'

'That's true I bet these coffee's probably cost a week's wages.'

Gheeta transferred her attention to a menu lying open on the coffee table. 'Four pounds sixty.'

Palmer was incredulous. 'One cup of coffee?'

'Yep, you could have had a side plate of six biscuits to go with it for another two ninety five if you liked.'

He nodded towards the street below the window. 'I bet there are people down there that don't spend that much on a day's food let alone six biscuits. How the other half live eh?'

'And die guv,' Gheeta sat back and looked around the luxurious lounge. 'I suppose if you are going to get murdered this place beats a back alley in Brixton.'

Palmer checked his wrist watch. 'Where's this manager bloke? Twenty past six already. We've been waiting for him to appear for forty minutes now.'

Gheeta reluctantly closed the magazine. 'Front desk said he was on his way.' She stood up and hoisted her shoulder bag which housed her laptop onto her shoulder. 'I'll go and hurry him up.' And off she went.

Palmer shifted forward in the chair and retrieved the case folder from the table flipping it open he began to refresh his mind on the case details so far.

Chapter 3

This was the third murder to take place in high class London hotels in six months. This time it had been a ballerina, before her an international model and a household name athlete had all been killed whilst staying overnight. The ballerina had been thrown from her hotel suite window, the model stabbed and slashed to death and the athlete strangled by her own tights. All had been investigated by their local CID units but nothing had been found to link them. No motive, no clues and no reason. Families, friends and business associates had all undergone serious questioning but still nothing. Nothing to link them together other than they all met their end in a London hotel room. A very expensive London hotel room and each body had a similar small piece of paper nearby with the name of a day and the word *'child'* written on it in the same hand. It seemed as though each murder had been carried out by an assailant acting on the spur of the moment against a random victim. Except that those pieces of paper and the names on them pointed to a planned murder not a random one. So Palmer knew this would not be random either. Thirty seven years as a copper had taught him that these things are never random. The theory of chaos didn't apply to crime. Somewhere there would be a pattern, a link, a reason. It was just the small matter of finding it. The only link so far was the pieces of paper with the name of a day and *'child'* written on them. When he'd seen the different reports of the murders coming across his desk at the Yard from the different forces CID crime updates he'd taken a second look and decided it was obvious they matched a serial crime profile. The reports were from different CID units so nobody had seen them all grouped together and recognised the paper link. He'd taken his thoughts up to the fifth floor at the Yard to his immediate boss Assistant Commissioner Bateman and asked for the cases to be transferred to the Serial Murder Squad.

He wasn't a fan of Bateman and Bateman wasn't a fan of Palmer. If he felt the need Palmer would use his years on the force and his record of solving crimes to ignore some of the new procedures and protocols ex university fast tracked suits like Bateman on the fifth floor wanted to bring in. Bateman on the other hand thought Palmer an old fashioned stickler who would block his modernising ideas or at least side step them in his own department if he possibly could. Twice he'd managed to get the Force to offer Palmer early retirement and twice Palmer had told them to take a running jump or words to that effect. So they just about tolerated each other avoiding contact wherever possible. But Bateman had the sense to appreciate Palmer's years of experience and his ability to use his hard gained knowledge and 'copper's nose' to back him when he presented a good reason for doing something. Palmer's wish to take over the unsolved hotel murders, which seemed to have hit the buffers, offered Bateman two opportunities. One, that the case would be solved and he could take credit for transferring it to Palmer's Squad, or two, it would fail and he could attribute its failure to Palmer losing his touch and ready for another offer of early retirement.

Chapter 4

Palmer shifted uncomfortably in the hotel lounge chair. He was getting very irritated now at the long waiting time. He knew Mrs P had made a steak and kidney pie for the evening meal and he intended to be there for it. He also knew she would have made him extra gravy which soaked into her pastry and gave his taste buds a real treat!

A clap of thunder so near that it sounded like it was coming from the floor above preceded a fresh torrent of rain outside. A couple of warm days to follow this lot and the grass in his garden would be growing at a foot a minute and Mrs P would be hinting that he should get the mower out. A chore guaranteed to set off his sciatica. He smiled to himself. *His* garden indeed! He wouldn't know a petunia from a pansy Mrs P was the garden expert. Between her and her green fingered friends at the local Gardening Club they could amass enough gardening knowledge to run Wisley. But he did do the hard stuff, the digging, the mowing and the hedge cutting. He didn't really mind that. Mrs P had created a lovely mature garden over the years and he had to admit, he did so enjoy a long summer evening on the recliner with a pint of Old Speckled Hen, some cashew nuts and a good book as the various scents of the garden wafted by. It was worth a few sharp stabs of sciatic pain and was as near a perfect end to a day as he could imagine. Waiting in a London hotel lounge for a manager to appear wasn't. With a great effort he pitched himself forward out of the chair's clutches and gathering the files made off towards the reception area on the ground floor. He took the lift down rather than maybe aggravate his sciatica on the stairs. It always seemed to be worse in wet weather.

Exiting the lift on the ground floor he crossed the large foyer to the front reception counter where he could see Sergeant Singh stood behind it talking on an internal phone. Her free hand was waving in the air as she underlined her points.

Five receptionists, two male, two female and one Palmer wasn't sure about, worked quickly and efficiently behind the long, busy counter which was holding at bay a three deep wave of guests. Keyboards clicked away as new guests booked in and PDQs whirred as those departing settled their bills.

A commotion at the front main doors caught his attention as he reached the counter. A middle aged, rather rotund, to put it politely, female celebrity of some kind was being ushered through a cluster of autograph hunters and other rubber neckers by two doormen. Two bell boys followed pushing an overloaded baggage trolley piled high with what seemed a perilous mountain of designer luggage cases that seemed about to topple over at any second. It occurred to Palmer that whoever this celebrity was, and he wasn't well versed on celebrities, she wanted people to know she had arrived. Being inconspicuous was not on this lady's agenda. Bright orange hair piled like an Eiffel tower topped an over painted face housing a crimson enhanced pair of lips and glinting white teeth which must have cost a fortune. They flashed brilliantly white through wide smiles given in all directions. A bright scarlet ankle length satin dress shimmered beneath a flowing jet black cape that swirled behind her as she was ushered into a waiting lift being held for her by another bell boy. And then she was gone. Palmer smiled to himself as he remembered an old Max Miller gag 'is your sister at home with Cinderella?' It takes all sorts.

He caught the eye of a female desk clerk and nodded towards the lift. 'Anyone I should know?'

The clerk raised her eyes to the Heavens in an exasperated look. 'Madame Geneelia, mystic, fortune teller and medium to the stars. Makes a mint predicting disasters and makes our life a misery when she's here.'

Palmer shrugged ignorance. 'Never heard of her, do you think if I asked her nicely she might be able to tell me what time your ruddy manager is going to appear or would that be too far in the future for her to forecast?'

The sarcasm was lost on the clerk who was saved from any more of Palmer's caustic tongue by Sergeant Singh's intervention from the far end of the counter. Covering the phone's mouthpiece she called across. 'On his way now Sir, apologises for the delay but definitely on his way.'

Best Sergeant he'd ever had was D.S. Gheeta Singh. An untapped Information Technology genius that he'd had transferred from the Yard's systems data team into his squad after being tipped off about her capabilities by his old mate George Frome in Forensics after she'd re-calibrated his computer analysis systems single handed. Palmer might be an 'old school' copper at heart but he was astute enough to know his department needed to be ahead of the game with computer technology and the benefits it brought to his team. He had called in a favour or two to check her CV and it was obvious that had Gheeta gone into a civilian systems and software development company she'd be on ten times the D.S. salary and that told him that she, like him, had been bitten by the bug that all policemen and police women have deep inside them, she wanted to catch villains. It was also obvious that she needed a challenge and stimulant to keep her satisfied with police work and his department had given her that and now four years down the line and with the minimal funding that Palmer could shift her way she had written a full analysis software programme that eclipsed the old HOLMES system plus many bespoke 'add-ons'. Programmes that checked and cross checked data in seconds and threw up any threads or coincidences. The basic building blocks of police investigation work. She had installed direct access intranet lines into all the public and government information networks that the department might need for cross referencing clues including Registry Office main frame, Land Registry, DVLC, local government and council electors lists, credit ratings bureaux and many more. Most were legal but Palmer was not daft and knew some were hacked into with their passwords proving no match for Gheeta, and some of those would probably need a Magistrate's order to look into if he went through the proper channels. But the 'proper channels' took ages and when you are dealing with serial killers you don't have ages.

Gheeta had enlisted a civilian computer operator called Claire to do the data input work and checking of the reference bases. Palmer nicknamed her 'JCB' because 'she just keeps digging away'. JCB was late twenties, married to a young city slicker and she and Sergeant Singh held long conversations in computer jargon that sidelined Palmer like a cat lover at Crufts. He had no idea what a zip file, hard copy or IPS was and always thought his mailbox was the hole in his front door not something floating up on a Microsoft Cloud, whatever that was.

Claire answered to DS Singh and competently managed the team room across the corridor from Palmer's office when the pair of them were out on a case like today. If needed a quick call to Claire for information would soon have reams of the relevant material downloaded through DS Singh's mobile onto her laptop for Palmer to read. Checks and counter checks could be done in seconds rather than hours or days. Yes, as investments go DS Gheeta Singh had been one of Palmer's best. Not quite as good as his Premium Bonds because he could get his money back off them but the saving in time and energy well made up for the money they'd spent on the systems.

He put the case files down as Gheeta came towards him and raised and inquisitive eyebrow as she joined him.

'He's on his way now Sir, had a problem in the kitchen apparently.'

'Good.' They moved to the end of the counter which seemed to be getting busier as residents returned from their day's business and joined the new arrivals at the check in, claimed their room keys, picked up any messages and made off to the row of lifts that seemed to be on a never ending yo-yo journey of ups and downs. The three main revolving doors from the street swished around continuously like big industrial machines disgorging wet guest after wet guest into the dry, warm, welcoming foyer of the Majestic.

'I am so sorry to have kept you waiting Chief Superintendent. Please forgive me.'

Palmer turned to find an early middle aged Hotel Manager approaching, smile in place, hand outstretched in friendship. Palmer took it and noticed a good firm grip which was a bit of a surprise. He'd always imagined hotel managers' handshakes to be, well, a bit limp.

The manager continued. 'Granger, David Granger I'm the manager of the Majestic.' He was, of course, as befits a hotel of this class, in the required black jacket over grey and black striped waist coat and trousers plus a shoe shine to blind you at fifty yards and large hand tied bow tie. It reminded Palmer of a 1940's film star. The brylcreemed jet black hair was the icing on the cake, too evenly black to be its natural colour, plus a manicured top lip moustache that sat atop a permanent smile. Dapper, that's the word thought Palmer. Flunky, that's the word thought Sergeant Singh. Palmer introduced himself and Sergeant Singh and they followed Granger behind the reception desk and through a door marked 'private' into an office, an office of luxurious opulence akin to the Guest Lounge upstairs. Granger shut the door behind them closing off the human noise and flopped into a large Captain's chair behind an equally large mahogany desk whilst indicating Palmer and Singh to take one of the various sofas available.

'Peace,' he said as he pulled at his bow tie and untied it to fall like a string of liquorice over his waistcoat. 'What a day, what a bloody awful day.' He pressed an intercom on the desk and barked into it at the voice that answered 'room service' politely. 'Janie it's Granger I'm in the reception office dear with guests. Be an angel and get us a pot of tea, a pot of coffee, three cups and plate of mixed sarnies. Quick as you can love, thanks.' he clicked off the intercom with a flamboyant jerk of the wrist. 'Right then Chief Superintendent, fire away, how can we help you?'

Palmer was surprised by the common London accent Granger had. He'd expected 'plum in the mouth' but detected a hint of cockney hiding behind the clipped sentences. 'Well Sir, first off we are probably going to bore you to tears. You see my department specialises in serial murders and….'

'Bore me?' Granger laughed. 'Chief Superintendent I spend hours and hours listening to rich, obese, over wealthy, extremely loud and utterly selfish people complaining that their mini bar hasn't the right brand of mixer or that room service took over ten minutes to deliver a freshly cooked meal at three in the morning or a similar triviality. If serial murders are boring compared to that lot, bore on, give me excess of it.' They all smiled.

'Twelfth Night eh?' Palmer's knowledge of the bard surprised Gheeta. It didn't surprise himself though as it was the only bit of Shakespeare he remembered having had to learn by heart for his English Lit. 'O' Level way back when exams counted for something, although that one hadn't because he'd failed it, but the lines had stuck with him. 'Well Sir, what I mean is that we will have to go back over all the information you and your staff have already gone through with the local CID. You see we have our own systems and unfortunately they come at a crime from a different angle to the CID systems. We need first hand information to programme into our data banks. Detective Sergeant Singh here is in charge of that side of the department and no doubt she'll be asking for lots of information.' He nodded towards Gheeta and passed her the ball.

Gheeta took over as she opened her laptop and clicked on. 'Access to your software is the first priority Sir, I'll need access to any computer files that refer to staff lists, staff shifts, guest lists, guest bills, including breakdowns and telephone calls made and received in the period of two months before the murder and a week after,' she smiled at Granger anticipating his concern. 'Don't worry sir we are covered by the Data Protection Act so any information we download will be kept on secure servers and destroyed once the case is closed. I'll need passwords to those files I've mentioned which I'll copy and send down line to our main frame so we can examine the files forensically without further disturbance to you.'

'Hmmmmm,' Granger pursed his lips. He was a bit apprehensive about having 'mister plod' trawling about in the Hotel's eighty thousand pound computer systems. No matter how attractive 'miss plod' was. 'I shall have to refer to head office for the go ahead on that one.'

Palmer threw him a false smile. 'Of course Sir, could you do that now so we can get started straight away? We have been here rather a long time already without any action so if there were to be a problem from your head office I'd have to get a couple of my chaps to pop round to the local magistrate for a seizure warrant and then we'll cart all your computers away and do it that way.' He flashed his *'so don't muck about with me sonny boy'* smile at a slightly taken aback Granger.

Sergeant Singh always had a job keeping a serious face on when Palmer did one of his quick changes. Mister nice guy could turn into Genghis Khan in the space of one sentence. Mind you he usually tried the 'nice guy' bit a little longer before bringing down the big hammer but this time he was obviously fed up with waiting so long for Granger to appear and wanted him to know in no uncertain manner that when it came to the crunch there would only ever be one winner. Palmer. What she didn't know of course was the thought of Mrs P's steak and kidney pie with extra gravy was also having its effect.

Granger shook his head as though to clear away cobwebs. 'Of course, of course superintendent, go ahead. You have immediate access to anything you need. We must get these awful murders cleared up or the London Hotel business will disappear. I didn't mean to be obstructive. It's been one of those days.' He threw Singh a glance. 'Please carry on feel free.'

Palmer relaxed. 'Right then, we've had three hotel guests murdered in their rooms at three different high class hotels. Got any ideas?'

Gheeta noted the 'can you help us' subliminal Palmer had just dropped in to get back on the 'nice guy' mode. 'Got to be an ex staff member with a grudge would you say?'

Granger inhaled. 'Possibly yes, but he or she would have to have one Hell of a grudge against three different hotels? We aren't even in the same Company group.'

Palmer agreed. 'Yes, and easier to burn them down than kill their guests, but why pick on the guests eh?'

'That's easy,' Granger felt good, he could offer an answer, 'No guests no business. So far the murders have been kept fairly quite in the press. A death in a hotel isn't news. Lots of wealthy elderly people take up residence in hotels. Some pass away so a press release from us about a resident's death would go unnoticed but a press release about one celebrity being bumped off would bring the house down let alone three being killed in different hotels.'

Palmer grunted. 'I must say you kept the lid on them, I had no idea about the deaths until the case was given to my department.'

Granger explained. 'The PR departments of the Hotels worked together to keep that lid firmly shut.'

'They've done a very good job. Right then what about your management structure here do you delegate?'

'Yes I do, well I do as much as I can. Although it doesn't seem to have much effect there are still not enough hours in the day. I've a front of house manager who runs the reception area, a security manager who tries to keep the thieves and call girls out, a property manager for maintenance and repairs, a housekeeping manager for keeping the rooms ship shape and clean....'

Palmer butted in 'Quite a few managers then?'

'Yes and they all have their under managers and staff to down delegate to as well.'

'Right, now if you wouldn't mind I'd like to take a look at the victim's room if I may and I'm sure Sergeant Singh would like a quick rundown of your PC systems.'

The hotel's Housekeeping Manager was summoned and led Palmer off to the second floor room whilst Granger set about familiarising Sergeant Singh with the hotels back office and book keeping systems which were fairly basic and took her all of five minutes to understand and plug in a USB to down load the lot. She'd then upload them onto the team computers at the Yard through her mobile phone for Claire to start running comparable software alongside and see what that might throw up.

'No use for old fashioned notebooks and pencils anymore then is there eh?' Granger made conversation as Singh worked.

'No Sir, far from it. It's all about information and speed of retrieval these days. Every clue we might find is usually on a computer somewhere.' She pulled out the USB. 'It's amazing when you think that your whole system is now copied onto this tiny chip.'

'Yes, amazing and quite worrying really, if it got into a competitor's hands...' he left the sentence unfinished.

'It won't Sir. And if it did they'd need the password. And three wrong goes at that and it wipes itself clean automatically.'

'How damn clever. Seems technology is taking us over Sergeant. Everything on Wi-Fi and no need for us humans at all.'

'Not quite at that point yet Sir,' she packed her shoulder bag. 'I think it's very likely you'll be seeing a lot of me and Detective Superintendent Palmer over the next few weeks and we are humans.'

Looking at DS Singh's deep olive skin, sharp trim features, large brown eyes and wide smile Granger didn't think that would be a bad thing. Not a bad thing at all.

Chapter 5

From the open window of the dead Ballerina's room on the seventh floor the pelting rain caught on the swirling winds between the high buildings seemed to be coming up from the street rather than down from the sky making Palmer's face a target as he leant out. Pulling his head back into the room to avoid it he closed the window. Traces of graphite left on the handle by the forensic boys brushing for finger prints smudged onto his hand. He wiped it off on the bed duvet much to the annoyance of Mrs Drummond the housekeeper who Granger had detailed to accompany Palmer to the room as she had been the one to find the body. She pursed he lips and forced herself not to point out the existence of a bathroom complete with soap, water and towels which would have been preferable to the duvet.

In her early sixties Mrs Drummond was past retirement age but had been persuaded to stay on by the Majestic management as her hand on the tiller of perhaps the most stressful and difficult job in any Hotel had always been a firm one. Her no nonsense attitude made sure it all ran very smoothly. Linen was changed on time, rooms cleaned and vacuumed until spotless, nothing less would do, bathrooms gleamed and even the fruit in the bowl got a wipe over. She took no prisoners, staff or guest, and had a stamina and fitness that belied her years. The only clue to her age was the grey hair knotted into a schoolmam's bun atop her thin face.

She'd taken an instant liking to Palmer as they travelled up in the lift chatting but after he had wiped his hands on the duvet it was quickly dimming. He was one of the old school and she liked that, noticing the shine on his shoes, the crease in his trousers and a clean white shirt. What she didn't know of course was that without Mrs P's intervention each morning Palmer would most probably resemble one of the dossers who made their home under a bench in the Royal Park opposite the Hotel every night and solicited her for a 'spare a bit of change missus?' as she made her way to the Underground Station on her way home.

She stood as straight as a pike staff in her green surge hotel trouser suit, the high collar of the white blouse held by a gilt clasp in the shape of the Hotel initials MH. An enamelled lapel badge gave her name and position and her pass key hung on a chain from a wide belt. Elegant had been Palmer's first impression.

He waggled the window too and fro. 'Take a bit of an effort to chuck a body out of that gap wouldn't it, even a thin ballerina's body.'

'It was open. The lock had been opened we closed it after the police had finished.'

'I see,' he said as he peered closely at the lock. 'Standard serrated barrel key. Buy them at any hardware shop not very secure is it?'

She smiled a 'pass the buck' smile. 'Security isn't my department Superintendent.'

'Chief Superintendent.'

Granger and Sergeant Singh entered the room.

'I've finished with the computers for now sir and sent it all down line to Claire.' Gheeta sat on the bed as she opened her laptop. 'Anything of interest here to note Sir?'

'No not really.' He pulled the window tight shut and shot the catch across. 'Do we know if the girl was dead before she was thrown out of the window?'

Gheeta pressed a few keys to bring up the autopsy reports on the victims and scrolled down to that of the ballerina's.

'She was killed by the impact of the fall Sir.'

'No medicine or drugs in the stomach?'

More scrolling of the screen. 'None found Sir. Nothing unusual at all in the PM.' She turned to Granger and Mrs Drummond and explained. 'Post mortem.'

Palmer turned away from the window brushing the rain from his jacket sleeves. 'Inside job then Sergeant, inside job.'

Granger and Mrs Drummond both stiffened and looked at each other in a startled way. DS Singh was used to Palmer's ways and knew that a copper bottomed explanation would follow. It did.

'This victim let the killer into her room and then let him or her heave her out of the window without a fight and according to the post mortem she was neither sedated nor under any drug related influence at the time. She was quite happy to let him or her in, to let him or her open the window wide and then let him or her throw her out. No signs of a struggle, no scuffle marks, no sliding prints on the window frame or ledge where she might have tried to grab hold. Nothing, so that would all point to the killer being a person she knew or somebody in authority that she was quite happy to let into the room. No forced entry and exactly the same in the other two cases. Could have been you Mrs Drummond.'

Mrs Drummonds mouth fell open but no words came out . Palmer fixed her with a steel look.

'Well she knew you didn't she. She was a regular guest. You could have come in on the pretence of airing the room, changing the curtains even. The poor girl wouldn't question you would she? All you have to do is open the window wide with your key, call her over to look at the view and as she leans out grab her ankles and whoops-a-daisy she's over the sill and gone.'

Mrs Drummond's mouth fell further open as she struggled for words. 'But….b…..but I can assure you...I...I…I never….'

Palmer relaxed her with one of his killer smiles. 'It wasn't you Mrs Drummond don't fret I was just illustrating my point that she must have known the murderer which is why it was an inside job meaning somebody inside her social circle, somebody she knew and trusted. Let's face it the girl wouldn't let a complete stranger into her room would she? And whoever it was came prepared with a window key and knew what type was needed. So could quite possibly be a member of staff.'

Granger had gone quite pale. 'So we could have a killer on our payroll?'

'You could have Sir. Glad I'm not staying here tonight.'

Chapter 6

In the squad car Palmer had requested to drop him and Sergeant Singh home she turned to him and shook her head in an unbelievable manner.

'What?'

'You know 'what' guv. All that about the killer might be a member of the Hotel staff. No way. Not unless he's got a job at three different Hotels and has a grudge against three major celebrities from three different walks of life. Poor Mrs Drummond, she'll be suspicious of all the staff now and Granger will be at his wits end worrying that he'll have another dead guest turning up'

Palmer smiled. 'Well perhaps I was a little over the top but he did keep us waiting an awful long time. And in any case I may be right. Claire might turn up a part timer that was working in each Hotel on the days in question.'

Chapter 7

After dropping Gheeta off at her apartment block the squad car dropped off Palmer at his Dulwich home a little after midnight. The lights were out so Mrs P must have gone to bed. He turned up his coat collar against the rain as he walked quickly up the short gravel drive and let himself in.

Raising herself lazily from her usual sleeping position, which was curled up on the hall carpet at the foot of the stairs, his faithful dog Daisy the English Springer made the effort and wagged her tail in greeting. Palmer gave her a pat, removed his shoes, trilby hat and coat and went into the kitchen with the dog in tow closing the door silently behind them.

First port of call was the microwave where his steak and kidney pie with the extra gravy sat invitingly. He pressed the buttons and watched for a moment as the inside lit up and the pie started to appetisingly revolve. Taking a can of Speckled Hen from the fridge he pulled a Windsor chair out from under the old pine farmhouse table and poured a glass of the nectar as he waited for the microwave to 'ping'.

A scribbled note along the edge of the day's newspaper lying on the table told him not to leave the dog in the kitchen. She had a habit of knocking over the swing bin in search of a midnight feast. It also told him that George was the final choice their second son and daughter-in-law had settled on for the imminent addition to the Palmer family. He'd quite forgotten all about that with the murders case taking over his thoughts. The hospital scan had shown that

Palmer was about to have another grandson. So now
the original list of ten first names that had been cut to
five was now down to one. George. That seemed
okay to Palmer. He had purposely stayed clear of the
arguing and choosing of the name. Whatever the kid
was going to be called he wouldn't like it. Who does
like their own name? Palmer certainly didn't. Justin.
What sort of name is that to give a boy? All those
years of schoolboy jokes about 'Justin time', 'Justin
case' and the rest. Still, George was all right. Good
old English name. Sounded sort of rock solid. No
rude connotations sprang to mind.

He raised his glass. 'Here's to you young George.'

The Palmers had three sons and a daughter, All
flown the nest. Place seemed very quiet now
compared to what it was when they were all bouncing
round it like beetles in a jar squabbling and growing
up. He smiled at the memory. Good times. And like
all good times they were over all too quickly of
course. But now he was a proud grandad to six boys,
soon to be seven and two girls. He liked kids. Mrs P
said he was still one himself at heart. Probably was
too. He certainly felt more like sixteen than sixty
plus.

A sharp 'ping' announced his steak and kidney was
ready and he tucked in under the jealous upward gaze
of Daisy who had perfected such a sad look to put on
when humans ate that any visitors that came round
for a meal melted immediately and furtively passed
her something under the table when Mrs P wasn't
looking. Palmer flicked his foot and gave her a
playful tap on the rear end. 'Hop it scrounger, you've
had yours.'

Thirty minutes later, fed, watered, washed and in his pyjamas he slipped into bed beside the familiar outline of Mrs P still thinking of how grandson George's life would be completely different to his.

Police work has taken Palmer into some of the worst socially deprived areas of the UK and he hadn't seen any improvement over the years, quite the reverse in some cases. The gap between the 'haves' and 'have-nots' had widened considerably since Thatcherism and its years of elitist plunder. The theft of the public sector that had been sold off to asset stripping friends of the Establishment rankled with Palmer every time he had a train cancelled or an incredibly high utilities bill. Cabinet Ministers retiring on fantastic pensions to take a highly remunerated seat on the board of companies they'd sold the nations treasure to or sitting their fat backsides onto a Commissioners position in the overblown workforce of the EEC. If England had been a South American country Palmer was sure there would have been coups and social unrest long ago. He'd written a paper about it for the Home Office 'think tank' that tried to plot the nations policing needs in the future. He had underlined the fact that if you take any comparable model from overseas societies it wouldn't be too long before the 'have nots' realised the 'haves' were never going to share and when the powder keg ignited the blast would be so big the thin blue line would be blown away. He'd given a talk some time ago in a side meeting at the Police Federation Conference on how he felt they were becoming a rich peoples' protection force rather than a law keeper. It went down well with his colleagues many of whom echoed his views but did not have Palmer's nerve to speak out. Calling a spade a spade and kicking 'political correctness' up the backside was something that had never troubled him and was a fault in his makeup that Mrs P had time and time again told him to reign in. A meeting with a Deputy Commissioner and a Home Office Official had quickly followed his Federation talk to underline that his views hadn't gone down very well with the top brass at the Home Office. Quite the opposite in fact and he had been told in no uncertain terms that had that talk found its way into the public domain and the tabloids had got hold of it the repercussions could have split the force and almost certainly meant enforced early retirement for Palmer. The meeting had been fairly ugly as were most of his meetings with the top brass. He gave as good as he got as he didn't like veiled threats of any kind. Anyway the future was for young George's generation to work out and try to keep a lid on. But for Palmer there was the little matter of three bodies in three hotels to sort out. He sighed loudly as his head hit the pillow.

'Justin,' Mrs P murmured half asleep.

'Yes my dear?' It might be his lucky night!

'I hope you did the washing up.'

It wasn't.

Chapter 8

D.S. Gheeta Singh had arrived home to her 7th floor
Barbican flat a little before eleven thirty.
Kicking off the clunky regulation shoes and swapping
her uniform for a loose bath robe she peered down
from the large picture window to the Thames snaking
past far below like a shimmering brocade in the night
light of London. The suburban lights of South
London out past the opposite bank bounced their
orange hue off the low, rain filled dark clouds. She
took a cool drink of orange from the fridge together
with a fruit salad and settled down in front of her
computer to check e-mails.

  Gheeta Singh's parents had been thrown out of
Uganda by Idi Amin and fled to the UK where they
started what had grown into a very successful
electronics company now run by her two brothers.
The whole family, most of who were in India, were
linked by their own website that Gheeta had built
herself which was basically a private chat room. Type
in 'hello mum' on the pc in her flat and there it was
on about eighty different screens throughout India,
the UK and New York where her uncle had fled to.
The site was very carefully password encrypted for
privacy and had, in the past, hosted many family
business meetings, birthdays and a few rows. No
traffic on the site tonight though just a few posted
questions for her to read. Cousin Barvinda in Dehli
wanted to know if she could get a 'Frozen' doll as
they were all sold out in India. Now that request
would have confused Palmer. Gheeta smiled at the

thought of him asking the staff at Iceland if they had one in stock. Her aunt was currently online having an argument with her grandma about Gheeta's age. Was she twenty nine or thirty? Which ever it was she should be married by now was her aunts point and she had a list of suitable Indian gentlemen of class who Gheeta should meet. Lately her aunt's life's work seemed to be trying to arrange a marriage for Gheeta. Every conversation with her ended up along that same thread which was why Gheeta avoided contact by using the 'secret' button when on the family site so she could eavesdrop without them knowing she was online. There was some earlier traffic between her brothers and an uncle in Dehli about getting some micro chips and motherboards sourced cheaply and that was it. She messaged Barvinda that she'd see what she could find about 'Frozen' dolls and logged off.

Usually she'd go over the day's work on her laptop and arrange it all chronologically but it had been a tough day and tonight the lure of her comfy bed was too much so after a quick shower she was soon sandwiched between mattress and duvet and fast asleep. Tomorrow would be a very busy day.

Chapter 9

Palmer's Serial Murder Squad offices were on the
fourth floor of New Scotland Yard. They consisted of
his office which he shared with DS Singh on one side
of the corridor and his operations room, known as the
Team Room on the other side. This room housed all
the computer terminals, servers and peripheral
software add-ons that DS Singh had set up originally
in the office which they had soon outgrown and so
had been moved over along with the arrival of Claire.
Claire had been a civilian data clerk that Gheeta had
noticed with her head buried in a computer magazine
one tea break at the Yard and in conversation had
found out that Claire was heavily into computing and
taking a degree in programming through an evening
class. A quick word in Palmer's ear and Claire was
transferred to his department where she took to the
back office work like a duck to water. Give her a
problem and Claire would dig away until she found
the answer. Hence Palmer had nicknamed her 'JCB'
which had stuck amongst the team. The team being
up to thirty officers seconded to Palmer on an ad hoc
basis when needed.

  He had called up twelve of them for a team meeting
for ten thirty in the Team Room and a hubbub of
noise spilling out from it met him as he crossed from
his office. Taking up his usual position in front of a
large 'write on wipe off' case progress board on
which DS Singh had blue tacked the three victims
photos and crime scene text he held up a hand for

silence. DS Singh sat at the side of the room. Claire worked away at her keyboard.

'Good morning ladies and gentlemen nice to see you all back here again please be seated.' He screwed up his face against the scraping of steel chair legs on old lino as the team sat to the desks that formed a semi circle line in front of him.

'On the desks in front of you are the various Met. Divisional files of the murders. DS Singh has already put you into four teams of three so this is your work load. Teams one to three are victim analysis you'll find a file on your designated victim on the desk in front of you in the work folders. I want full backgrounds investigated, friends past and present, business circle, social interests, debts, bank accounts, just about anything you can find out. Each team has a laptop so put all the information you glean onto that and don't wait until you get back here to send it in. The idea of the laptop is so you download information as you get it in the field straight to Claire.' He paused for a moment whilst the officers opened their folders. 'The Divisional CIDs have had these cases for a couple of months so time is important as clues get cold and witness memories dim after a while. This is a live case ladies and gentlemen with nobody remotely in the frame yet. I think we'll probably find the victims to be clean but you never know so dig deep. Team four I want you three to work inside the Hotels. Try and get a temp job inside and see what the staff are talking about, what they are saying about the murders. If you can't get inside find out where staff go for lunch and get talking with them there. Find out who hates who and why in the managerial structures on the Hotels. Keep scratching.' He turned to look at the victims pictures on the board. 'We have three people here who innocently booked into a Hotel and left in a bodybag. All killed for no apparent reason and maybe at random. The only link between them is they were murdered in a Hotel and each time the killer left a piece of paper with the name of a day written on it. But you and I ladies and gentlemen know that there will be a greater link. So go find it.' He rubbed his hands together in a workmanlike manner. 'Right then usual communication lines apply, all information into JCB via the laptops, no post-it notes or text messages and all operational queries through DS Singh.' He paused to check his watch. 'It is now eleven ten so study your folders and plan your operations and be out and on the job by one o-clock. And that includes having lunch. Claire is currently downloading as much information on your victims as she can get from Social Security, credit agency data and all other National data bases they appear on and she will have that downloaded onto your laptops in…..?' He turned to Claire with eyebrows raised questioningly.

'Twenty minutes max Sir.' Her eyes never left the screen as she answered.

'Excellent. Right then let's get on with it, let's get a result.' He smiled like a schoolmaster leaving a class in the exam room and returned to his office followed by DS Singh.

No sooner had they sat to their desks than Claire gave a perfunctory tap on the door and came in. She had a big smile on her face which Palmer noticed.

'You look like the cat that got the cream, what have you found?' He relaxed and pushed his chair, which could have come from any nineteen fifties office furniture supplier, back on its back legs until it jarred into the deep groove in the wall plaster dug out by this repeated action over the years. He clasped his hands behind his head. 'Come on don't keep us in suspense then.'

'The Majestic has nine illegal immigrants on its payroll. The other two hotels have about the same. None are registered with immigration or have national insurance numbers and all are being paid not by the Hotels but by an employment agency, the same agency in all three cases.'

Gheeta being the daughter of an immigrant was a little shocked. 'You'd think a company as big as the Majestic would have a few safeguards in place to check on who they were hiring wouldn't you?'

Palmer nodded negatively. 'No, not if they are outsourcing that check is up to the agency that they use. And cheap labour is cheap labour. I doubt if the illegals are going to complain are they. No doubt stuck in the kitchens out of sight, low profile, no hassle and some cash in hand at the end of the week.'

Gheeta wasn't happy. 'But the Hotel could have a whole terrorist cell working there and not know it.'

'I doubt it, probably just a few guys making a bit of money to send back to their poverty stricken families in some third world war zone. But stick to the rules Claire, copy the details to the AT (Anti Terrorist) department just in case so they can give them the once over.'

Claire nodded. 'What about HM Revenues and Taxes, copy to them?'

'No let them do their own dirty work. Why grass on some poor wretch who probably paid a king's ransom to get here and works his butt off for a few quid a week to keep his family from starving. They'd only get shoved into a detention centre which would cost us tax payers a fortune each week. I'd rather put some politically correct arsehole of a social worker who's never done a real days work in their life inside one.'

Gheeta smiled at Claire. 'All opinions expressed in this office are solely those of the person making them.'

They both laughed as Gheeta's phone rang.

'DS Singh can I help you?........hello mister Granger.......you're kidding...........okay don't touch anything we'll be right over.' She put the phone down and looked at Palmer.

His shoulders sagged. 'Another body?'

She nodded. 'With a note attached.'

'A note what kind, another 'child' note or a ransom note?'

'He didn't say.'

Chapter 10

Madame Geneelia did not look very nice dead. In fact she looked hideous. Death has a habit of stripping away the body cosmetic, the personality it once housed and leaving on view the basic flesh and shape helpless in its inadequacy to convey to the viewer even the slightest hint of the person it once housed. The person whose body it once belonged to has gone and now like an empty discarded pupa it is left behind, the empty host to an expired life.

Madame Geneelia's body minus Madame Geneelia was quite a shock to Palmer and Singh as they took their first look at it lying exposed on the hotel room floor. Madame Geneelia had obviously been dressed in only a bathrobe when she had opened her hotel room door to the killer who's vicious attack had sent her sprawling backwards onto the plush carpet where he or she had then repeatedly plunged a serrated steak knife into her ample chest which had presented itself as a suitable target when the robe had opened with the fall.

They stepped into the room with care so as not to disturb any forensic evidence that may be there. Palmer removed his trilby as a show of respect. Mister Granger was already there together with another gentleman that Palmer took to be another Hotel management person.

'Could we give her some dignity and cover the chest Sir?' Gheeta was embarrassed for the poor woman.

'Better not Sergeant, best let forensics do their work first. They'll be here soon. Anything been moved or touched in here since the body was found Mister Granger?'

'Nothing.' Granger was quite white. The blood over Madame Geneelia's chest and robe was making him feel queasy. 'Oh except this,' he pulled a written note from his pocket, 'It was on the body. I moved it when I felt for her pulse.' He offered it to Palmer who knew better than to add his fingerprints to the piece of paper which could yield substantial clues.

'What does it say?'

'Wednesday's child.'

'Is that all?'

'That's all yes.'

'Okay put it on the bedside table if you would Mister Granger. Anybody else handle it?'

'Only mister Dolland here.' Granger indicated the rather portly balding man standing behind him. 'It was inside an envelope which Mister Dolland opened.'

Dolland pulled an envelope from his pocket and gave it to Granger who added it to the paper on the side table.

'And Mister Dolland is?' Palmer wanted to know.

'Oh sorry Chief Superintendent I should have introduced you. Mister Dolland is our Head of Security.'

'Really, not doing very well at present are you Mister Dolland?' It was statement not a question. 'Two murders on the premises, somebody's getting in who shouldn't be.'

Dolland was embarrassed. 'No, well…..I mean…it's all a bit out of our league Chief Superintendent. We're usually catching room thieves and fraudsters.....murder isn't something I'm used to. It's awful, absolutely awful.'

'Yes, well, not a nice thing to happen at any time. Perhaps you'd make sure the room is untouched and let our DA people have the note and envelope when they arrive?'

'DA people?'

'Document Analysis, not an ex copper then Mister Dolland? Most Hotel security people are these days.'

'No, no...always been in the Private Sector, Securicor, G4 and others.'

Gheeta felt sure that had Dolland not been there Palmer would have voiced his well known low opinion about 'amateurs' in the Police and Security sectors.

The forensic team she had called in arrived together with a doctor to issue a death certificate.

Palmer could see no point in remaining. 'Right then Mister Granger the Sergeant and I will be off and leave it all in the capable hands of Forensics. Once they have finished our undertaker will come and remove Madame Geneelia to the police morgue for a pathologist to do a P.M. That's a post mortem Mister Dolland.' There was a sarcastic hint in his voice. 'I suggest this floor is emptied of guests and kept barred from the public and staff until I release it back to you Mister Granger. Can't think that any guest would want to have a room near a murder scene anyway and our people will be in and out for a couple of days and there will be an officer on the door at all times. We'll be in touch if we need anything. I'll put a media block on it at our end so you might want your PR people to spin something to the press Mister Dolland. It's bound to leak out now being two murders so I'd get going on that if I were you before all your bookings get cancelled. Unexplained death or something similar usually keeps the tabloid hounds at bay for a few days.' He put his trilby back on nodded to the pair of them and left with Sergeant Singh alongside.

'So Dolland isn't much of a Head of Security is he guv? I think I might check him out. Bit of a clown.'

'The whole Hotel is a Fred Karno's if you ask me Sergeant.'

'Fred Karno's?'

'Bloody circus. Make sure we get a copy of that '*Wednesday's Child*' note asap. Those notes with a day written on them are all we have at present that links the murders together. It's not much of a link,' he smiled excitedly at Singh. 'But we have a link.'

Chapter 11

The next morning Gheeta and Palmer stood behind the seated Claire in the team room looking at the text on the screen. Claire tapped the keyboard. 'Putting in the days referred to in the paper notes at the murders doesn't bring up anything except this text. It's an old children's poem.'

Gheeta read it aloud off the screen.

'Monday's child is fair of face.
Tuesday's child is full of grace.
Wednesday's child is full of woe.
Thursday's child has far to go.
Friday's child is loving and giving.
Saturday's child works hard for a living.'

Palmer commented. 'No *Sunday's child* then?'

Claire nodded. 'No the poem doesn't have a *Sunday's Child*'

'So if we take the notes on the bodies to be referring to this poem then we should get a match between the victim and the day? Can't mean anything else can it?' Palmer said.

Gheeta could see a double meaning. 'Okay but what's the key? Is the killer working through the days of the week murdering somebody for each day, in which case what about Sunday? Or is he or she working through the types of 'child' relative to the poem?'

'Both.' Claire was keying in facts and brought them up on screen. 'The victims tie in with the days. It makes sense, listen, *Monday's child is fair of face* has to be the model and she was killed on a Monday.

Tuesdays child is full of grace has to be the ballerina who was killed on a Tuesday, ballerina's are graceful. *Thursdays child has far to go* is the marathon runner and yesterday, Wednesday, *Wednesday's child is full of woe* is Madame Geneelia the mystic. Got to be that way, each line describes the victim *and* their day of death.'

'Two to go then,' Palmer stated the obvious. 'Friday and Saturday. Could be anybody couldn't it? *Friday's child is loving and giving…..*could be anyone, could be me.'

Gheeta and Claire both had a sudden coughing fit.

Palmer had expected that and continued with a slight smile. 'As could be *Saturday's child who Works hard for a living.'*

Gheeta sighed. 'Where do we start guv? It's too wide a pool of potential victims.'

'We carry on as we are Sergeant. Put everything into the computer programmes, just keep feeding it in and cross our fingers that we find a link. There will be one somewhere. This killer is killing for a reason and I don't think he or she has come across the poem and thought 'oh that's a nice thread to kill by', no, the victims were already lined up and the poem just fitted them perfectly. There will be a strong link between this poem and the victims, and there's an audience too.'

Gheeta was puzzled. 'An audience guv?'

'Of course, if you were the killer and were doing it for a personal reason for self gratification no need to leave a note is there? If the victims had done something to you and this was revenge you'd do the deed and move onto the next one. You wouldn't leave notes. No, this killer is playing to an audience, somebody or some people other than the killer know what's going on and the significance of the notes. He or she is saying to that audience '*look how good I am*' and to us '*come on copper you can't catch me.*'

'We usually do.'

'And we will this time too.'

'This is interesting.' Claire was scrolling down files on screen and brought one up. She half turned to Sergeant Singh. 'That Dolland chap you wanted a search on.'

Gheeta nodded. 'The Hotel security man.'

'Yes,' Claire studied the screen. 'There were some invoices in the Hotel accounts from an agency company called Central Recruitment who supply manual and catering staff to Hotels including the Majestic. Central Recruitment, according to their details lodged at Companies House has two directors, Evelyn and Robert Dolland.'

'Crafty bugger,' Palmer laughed. 'He's got it all worked out hasn't he eh? Talk about keep it in the family. I bet that's a nice little earner for him and the wife.'

'It is.' Claire scrolled a bit further. 'Their company accounts show they supply most of the other big name hotels too on a regular basis. The Hotels pay Central Recruitment who we assume pay the people they send. Last accounts, two years old, show a profit of seventy grand.'

'Hmmm' Palmer thought for a moment. 'I can't see a tie in with the murders though. Madame Geneelia would have known Dolland and let him in the room if he'd come knocking but the other victims in other

Hotels wouldn't. Put all that on the back burner Claire I think we are more likely to find links between the victims somewhere else along the line than anything Dolland is involved in. Anyway what he and his wife are doing is all legal and above board. Anything come up on the hotel guests? Be nice to find the same guest booked into each of the hotels on the murder nights.'

'I'm still running the programme Sir. Bit of a mammoth job that one but fingers crossed.'

The door opened and the portly frame of Reg Frome, Head of the Forensics department, came in holding up the latest note and envelope in an evidence bag.

Reg Frome and Palmer went back a long way together both joining the Met. from school with Reg taking the science path. He really did look like the mad scientist Doc Brown from the film Back to the Future with his hair permanently standing on end.

'Good morning all.'

'Aha!' Palmer was expectant. 'Come to give us some good news Reg? Fingerprints of a known villain all over the note I hope?'

Reg sat down. 'Not exactly Justin, but interesting. I gave it to my Document Analysis chaps and they say the handwriting is obviously faked with lots of lifts and stop-starts, no flow to it so whoever wrote it was doing their best to disguise it. It was very amateurish really. Don't know why they bothered. These days you can use any number of type faces and fonts on a basic computer and they can't be traced. Well they can but only if we get the hard drive and find the letter on it. Anyway, the prints are Granger's and Dolland's on the envelope and Grangers on the note. The note was folded so we would expect a partial print where the person who folded it had touched it but the clever sod used kitchen gloves. We know that because they have a high oil content which holds the colour pigment fast to the rubber base material in the manufacturing process. We can pick that up in an infra red scan.'

'Is that it?' Palmer was disappointed.

'Pollen.'

'Pollen?'

'Yes, very small traces of flower pollen from roses and chrysanthemums on both note and envelope.'

'Interesting.'

'And that's it Justin. Sorry. Waiting on a couple of other test results on all four notes but I'm pretty sure they'll come back negative too.' He rose to go. 'Sorry.'

'Okay Reg, thanks for taking a look so quickly, take care.' He sat back disappointed in his chair as Frome left with a nod to Claire and Gheeta. 'Well rubber gloves and pollen eh? It seems we are looking for a florist who does the washing up.' His disappointment at the forensic result showed in his voice.

'I think you might be wasting your time Sir,' Claire looked towards him dejectedly. 'Look at this.' She'd pulled up a colour crime scene picture of Madame Geneelia's room. The body, now covered, lay where it had fallen. 'Take a look at the bedside table sir.'

Palmer and Gheeta bent closer to the screen.

'Oh blast,' Palmer exhaled loudly. The picture showed the letter and envelope on the bedside table where Granger had put them directly underneath a large vase of roses and chrysanthemums. 'Back to square one then eh? Mind you well done for spotting it Claire I'd have looked a right fool if I'd got the team out interviewing every florist in London wouldn't I eh?'

'Hang on, that reminds me.' Gheeta lent towards the screen. 'Pull up the crime scene pictures of the murdered model please Claire.' A few keyboard clicks later and there they were in a page of small icons. Gheeta studied them closely and pointed to one. 'Pull that one up.' It was similar to the Madame Geneelia picture. A Hotel room with a body lying on its back on the floor, the face had been attacked with a vengeance.

'Not a pretty sight.' Palmer grimaced.

'It's the tee shirt guv her tee shirt has writing on it. I meant to take a look before but Madame Geneelia's murder made it slip my mind. Can you get a better image Claire?'

Claire could. A few clicks and zooms later and the logo letters MCDA were clearly visible on the blood stained tee shirt.

'What's MCDA then?' Palmer wanted to know. He guessed it would be some fashion logo being promoted by the model.

Gheeta was stumped. 'No idea guv.'

'Me neither,' Claire hadn't seen it before, 'but give me a minute and I'll find out.' She keyed the letters into her computer. 'Here we are, Multiple Criteria Decision Analysis….?' She looked enquiringly at Palmer and Gheeta.

'I can't see that has any relevance to modelling?' Gheeta was puzzled.

'No.' Palmer agreed. 'It's not going to be that, whatever *that* is. Give the team covering her murder a bell and get them to ask the Victim Support Officer who's with her family to have a quiet word and see if they can help. It could be some local club she belonged to.'

His phone rang across the corridor in his office. 'Hey up. Here we go. Let's hope it's not *Fridays Child* been knocked off a day early!'

'I'll get it guv,' said Gheeta and made her way quickly to the office and picked up the phone. 'Superintendent Palmer's office Sergeant Singh speaking can I help you?.......hello Mrs P how are you.....still waiting the new addition then eh?....okay, hang on he's here now.'

Palmer came in and took the phone, 'Hello Princess, I take it that George is taking his time eh?.......well don't worry I seem to recall one of ours kept us waiting for three days.........you're getting what? Spike? What's 'spike'..... oh Skype.....on the computer.....what's that for?......why do you need to see them you call the kids near enough every night as it is and spend hours on the phone, you don't need to see them on the telly as well......who?......oh I might have known Benji would have it, so what, doesn't mean we need it just because Benji has it.'

Benji, full name Benjamin was Palmer's next door neighbour. A retired advertising executive in his early sixties, spray on tan, pony tail, designer clothes and in Palmer's estimation, of questionable sexual orientation. Too much money and too much time on his hands was Palmer's usual 'Benji' mantra. Three or four continental cruises or holidays a year, a new motor every year and Palmer reckoned a new nip and tuck every year too. Benji was a great favourite with most of the ladies in the area, especially Mrs P. and her gardening club and WI friends, and this rankled a bit with Palmer who was their favourite until Benji moved in and knocked him off top spot.

'How will it possibly save us money? Those solar panels were going to do that….we had to have them after 'Benji' had them installed on *his* roof..…..yes I know they will eventually ….eventually being about twelve years time! And then only if we're lucky and the government still wants to buy electricity of us by then. Be better off doing some fracking under the garden…..now that's an idea!' He winked at Gheeta. 'I'll get a fracking company to drill down and then turn right and go under Benji's garden and do some fracking there…..with a bit of luck it'll loosen the rock and cause a sink hole and he'll fall into it and never to be seen again….….what do you mean he's at the door now? What for?........to help you download the Skype?…..get the chap from the TV shop round to do it……I don't care if it is easy to do…and if it is why has Benji got to come round to do it……I'm not being silly…..okay….yes, yes, see you later normal time if nothing crops up this end…… okay…love you too.' He put the phone down and slumped into his chair and exhaled loudly. 'Apparently we are now going to be in visual contact with all the family through the computer linked to the telly by a thing called Skype. So no prizes to guess where Mrs P will be sat all evening….every evening.'

'Cheer up guv it will save you money there's no charge for it so your phone bill will go down if she uses it instead of the phone.'

'Sergeant it is a given in my life that nothing Mrs P does saves me money. Right then.' He shifted his mind back to the case. 'Where do we go from here, can't just sit and wait for another victim? There's a tie up somewhere between these murders and I'm blowed if I can see it other than the bits of paper and names of days.'

The office door opened and Assistant Commissioner Bateman popped his head round. Bateman was the complete opposite to Palmer and they often crossed swords. The last time being when Bateman tried to transfer Sergeant Singh away from Palmer into the newly formed Cyber Forensics Department, a move neither Palmer nor Gheeta wanted. A compromise had been found after a lot of threats and counter threats. The only threat Palmer could not use was to threaten to resign as Bateman would jump at the opportunity to get rid of him. Bateman was a Commissioned Officer out of university with degrees in everything and experience in nothing. Palmer compared him to Politicians, *'Never had proper jobs and think they can run the country.'* Bateman was obvious material for the top floor executive offices being forty five years old and folically challenged, or in Palmer speak *'bald as a badger's arse'* and with a liking for focus groups, departmental mission statements and other management tools that Palmer had never heard of let alone participated in that set the two of them well apart in their ideas of how modern policing should be carried out. He nodded to Sergeant Singh.

'Just passing so I thought I'd check on the Hotel murders case Palmer? How's it going? Any leads?'

'None so far Sir, doesn't seem to be any links between the victims except bits of paper left at the murder scenes, but we know there must be one or two more somewhere. Bit of a brick wall unless you know what MCDA stands for?'

'Multiple Criteria Decision Analysis.'

Palmer was taken aback. 'Blimey.'

'It's a way modern management differentiate between a number of decisions that could be taken on a problem to assess the effect each might have. What has that to do with this case?'

'One of the victims had those initials printed like a logo on a tee shirt that she was wearing.'

Bateman frowned. 'Interesting, but I wouldn't think they stood for that, bit obscure. I would think it more likely to be the initials of a pop group or similar.'

'We can't find a match anywhere. We are getting the Victim Support Officer to ask the family if they can shed any light on it.'

'Good idea, okay keep me in the loop.' Another perfunctory nod to all and he was gone.

'Keep him in the loop guv,' Gheeta mocked. 'Better add him to your Skype friends and you would be able to chat to him from home and bring him up to date each evening. You'd like that.'

'The only loop I'd want to keep him in is one hanging over a gibbet!'

'Why didn't you tell him about the link to the poem?'

'Take too long explaining it and he'd only ask for a written update and we can't spare the time for that.'

Chapter 12

George duly arrived in the world that evening and as Palmer cradled his latest grandson in the hospital ward with Mrs P and the rest of the family cooing and tickling his cheek, George's that is, not Palmer's…he couldn't help thinking of the future and where *this* little 'Wednesday's child' would plough his furrow. Would he follow grandad into the police? Probably not, none of the other Palmer children had and none of the grandchildren were showing any interest either. If the standard issue weapon of the Force was a Star Wars Light Saber instead of a baton they would probably be interested. Other than that his mind was continually churning over what was likely to be the killer's next move.

Friday and Saturday passed uneventfully as far as any new bodies turning up in hotel rooms was concerned. So *Friday's Child* and *Saturday's Child* seemed to be safe for another week but Palmer couldn't help thinking that perhaps these murders weren't related to the poem and it was just a coincidence that the victims' professions matched their death days in the poem. Trouble was that if you let your brain struggle with that conundrum it began to hurt. Palmer knew from experience to keep his mind focused on the 'modus operandi' of the crime and to keep to the well proved method of feeding Sergeant Singh's computer programs with every snippet of information about the victims and the crimes they could find and that process would, sooner or later, come up with a viable lead. Reciting a poem wouldn't do that. Information, information, information was a well worn Palmer mantra that was in his book the basic of all Police work and far better than an aching brain trying to work out riddles.

Chapter 13

'We have lift off guv!' An excited Gheeta bounced into the office from the team room.

It was Monday, half way through the morning and Palmer sat at his desk, his chair leaning back onto the wall, feet on the desk looking through the crime scene photos yet again for anything he might have missed when he looked through them the other dozen times over the weekend.

Gheeta put a large family photo album on his desk as his chair came into the upright position with a bang that sent a sciatic needle of pain through his left thigh as he waited to be told what he was looking at.

'This guv is the model's family photo album. Our Victim Support Officer with them broached the subject of the MCDA tee shirt and guess what?' She opened the album to a page showing a large photo of a big group of teenagers many wearing similar tee shirts. 'The Milner College of Dramatic Art, class of nineteen eighty four,' she pointed to a figure, 'and there's our model.'

A large weight was beginning to move off Palmer's shoulders. 'Well, well, well, what a turn up,'

Gheeta was bubbling. She moved her finger to another figure. 'And there's our ballerina,' and her finger moved on to point at another, 'and that is Rosalind Kirby, or as we know her, Madame Geneelia.'

Palmer was smiling now. 'This is it then Sergeant, the missing link, the one thing they all had in common. MCDA, The Milner College of Dramatic Art.'

'And the class of nineteen eighty four guv.'

'Yes, so we might well be looking at *Friday's Child* and *Saturday's Child* in this very photo.'

'And maybe the killer too.'

'Right, we need some names and addresses is this college still going?'

Gheeta nodded. 'Yep, housed in a large Victorian residence off Red Post Hill, Herne Hill, and before you ask, the car I ordered to take us there should be waiting downstairs any minute now.'

'You know Sergeant,' Palmer joked thoughtfully as he took his Prince of Wales check jacket from the coat stand and perched his trilby on the back of his head, 'I'll make a copper out of you yet.'

Chapter 14

The Milner College of Dramatic Art was quite an
imposing four story red brick Victorian building in its
own grounds. A short, narrow, leafy drive led from
the main road to a crunching pebble turning circle in
front of wide stone steps leading up to a pair of
modern glass revolving doors. Inside it changed from
the Victorian facade to ultra modern with a large open
plan foyer, a reception desk and several rehearsal
rooms leading off.

  Gheeta had rung ahead and spoken to the Principal
Mr Hawley Timms-Beddis who greeted them with a
limp handshake and worried look and quickly ushered
them into his plush office.   He reminded Palmer of
Benji, sixty something going on thirty two in tight
jeans a skinny frame and a pony tail. He was clearly
upset by the news that his ex pupils had been
murdered.

  'It's dreadful, awful, absolutely awful'. He steadied
himself with a glass of what Palmer took to be brandy
from a tray of various bottles on the desk. Palmer
declined the offer of a glass for himself. Hawley
Timms-Beddis poured a refill. 'Are you sure I can't
get you anything Superintendent?'

  '*Chief* Superintendent, no, not whilst I'm on duty
thank you Sir.'

  'Oh sorry, yes of course, Chief Superintendent.' He
took a large gulp. 'I suppose same goes for you
Sergeant?'

  'Yes Sir, but thank you for the offer.'

'This news is awful, awful. I knew all those young ladies you know. I knew them all. I'd just started here as Assistant to the Principal Drama coach.' He took another large drink. Palmer thought he'd end up on the floor if he didn't slow down. 'Stars of the year they were. Well I mean look how well they all did, and then to be murdered. Oh how awful. Who could have done such a thing?'

'Well, that's why we are here sir,' said Palmer and held out his hand to Gheeta who pulled the Class of 1984 photo from her shoulder bag. Palmer passed it to Timms-Beddis who went distinctly white and took another large gulp of his drink.

'Oh no, no, no, no. You think one of our ladies is the murderer don't you? Oh no, oh my God.' He clasped his hands together in front of his chest as he gazed at the photo. 'The College will close. Nobody will want to enrol after this news breaks.'

Palmer was beginning to think that Timms-Beddis the ex Assistant Drama Coach was getting into character a bit now and thought about giving him a slap. He'd never had much time for 'theatrical luvvies' and their world. Mrs P liked the period dramas on television. Palmer hated them. *BBC has spent so much on the costume department they have to use them.* He'd argued. *Same old storyline, posh 'titled' family with large estate who's youngest son falls in love with local blacksmith's daughter…..panic in the family followed by murder, arson, a baby and an ending that leaves it open for a second series….hackneyed rubbish.* Was Palmer's considered view of most of the Beeb's drama department's output. And his opinion of the reality shows would make a Thames Docker blush. So Timms-Beddis's wringing of hands didn't get a caring reaction from Palmer just a quick memory of Charles Hawtrey in the Carry On films.

'You're jumping the gun a bit here Sir,' Palmer said and gave out one of his reassuring smiles. 'We are at a very early point in the investigation and just seeking information. There's no need for any of this to leave this room.'

Timms-Beddis was a little relieved at this. 'How can we help you?'

Gheeta took up the reigns. 'Do you have the roll call for nineteen eighty four on a computer or disk?'

Timms-Beddis was not the person to ask. 'I have no idea. We must have a record somewhere but it will be in the accounts section, I can ask them to look?'

Gheeta smiled. 'I think it best if you just take me along to the accounts section and let me do the asking. Be much quicker for me to explain what we need and I'm sure you'd like us to be as quick as we can and go away before tongues start to wag.'

She was learning fast thought Palmer.

Gheeta continued. 'Far easier if I download the information we need to work on and then we can take a detailed look at it back at our office. Are you agreeable to that?

'Yes of course.' Timms-Beddis just wanted them out of his College before tongues started to wag and new student applications started to flag.

Chapter 15

Miss Jacobs the Head of Accounts for the Milner College of Dramatic Art was far more help than Timms-Beddis. Although well beyond retirement age she displayed a calm outlook of complete control and Gheeta had warmed to her as soon as she had said, 'Oh my dear, don't bother with Timms-Beddis in future just come straight through to me. He may be the bees knees in the artistic community but like so many great men he has a great woman behind him.' She smiled sarcastically. 'Me.' She tapped at her keyboard. 'Class of nineteen eighty four you said, yes?'

'Yes please', Gheeta nodded. 'What information would you still have on them?'

'Well everything my dear, names, addresses, that is their addresses from back then. Of course most will have moved on by now. Married, divorced, become famous, sunk without trace or got a proper job,' she said and smiled at Gheeta. 'Lots of egos get crushed at a college like this.' Gheeta noticed that the computer screen was showing names, addresses, fees, certificates and a lot more.

Miss Jacobs inhaled loudly. 'Oh. It was *that* year was it, oh dear.'

'What do you mean *that* year'?'

'1984 is known as the *'problem'* year dear. Is that what this investigation is about?'

'Could be but it's just a general search for information on a couple of the year's students. Why, what was the problem?' Gheeta tried to appear uninterested but inside was bursting with anticipation.

'Well I wasn't employed here at that time, I started in eighty six but as far as I have gleaned over the years it was rather a nasty affair. One of the girls fell out of the sixth floor window of the props warehouse. That's a building behind this one. Poor girl was dead as soon as she hit the concrete.'

'She fell?'

'Maybe.'

'Maybe?'

'Suicide so the rumour mill has it. But the Coroner gave it as Accidental Death. But you can't open a window five foot above the floor and fall out of it can you?' She sat back in her chair. 'You see my dear all these girls come here with such great expectations. They all think they are the next Judy Dench and that Agents will be falling over themselves to sign them up and off they'll go to a life of stardom and riches. But it doesn't happen. This is a fee paying college so if mummy and daddy can afford the fees their offspring gets in, talented or not. No audition piece to be done, just a cheque to be signed.'

'You make it sound a bit tacky.'

'Not tacky my dear it's just business. At the end of the financial year there's a profit and loss account like any other business and so far we've been on the profit side of the page. Do you want a print out of this 1984 information?'

'No.' Gheeta took a data stick from her shoulder bag. 'I'll download it if I may? We have cleared it with Mister Timms-Beddis. Save a lot of time. '

'Of course, help yourself. Sit here.'

Sergeant Singh took over the chair as Miss Jacobs moved off it. She pushed the data stick into a side

USB port and hit the keys. In a few seconds the green line on the download box on the screen was moving across at speed as the information passed from the hard drive to the stick. And then it was done.

'That's it all done. Bit faster than printing off pages.
'

'Too right my dear. I may be of an age that was brought up on the typewriter and carbon paper but I love the new technologies. Accounts and spread sheets on the computer, click click done.'

Gheeta laughed. 'I get the impression Miss Jacobs that the Milner College of Dramatic Art might well grind to a halt were you to retire.'

'Retire? Me? Don't mention that word. If forty is the new twenty my dear then seventy is the new thirty five. Do I look a bit too old for thirty five?' She laughed.

Gheeta was well pleased with the way she'd handled Miss Jacobs. Everything she wanted and more was now on the data stick nestling in her shoulder bag. So the class of nineteen eighty four had been disrupted by a student's unusual death. Interesting seeing as three more had met the same fate recently.

Chapter 16

It was late in the day so Palmer decided to wait until the next day, Tuesday, to start looking in depth at the '*class of nineteen eighty four*'. He sat at a desk in the Team room leafing through the ballerina's photo album again as Sergeant Singh and Claire hit the computer programmes and uploaded the Milner College information. Names, addresses, and anything else about the students of that year went in to be analysed, compared and sifted.

'It's all very straightforward stuff Sir.' Gheeta shook her head in a resigned manner, 'nothing exciting popping out of the information. They seem to be a very boring class.'

Palmer looked up from the photos. 'Nothing about suicides then no name disappearing off the roll after half the year?'

'Quite a few didn't make the full year but no reasons given. Could have been a number of reasons I suppose. Maybe they didn't make the grade. Mummy and daddy may have run out of cash. Maybe they found that a career in the arts just wasn't for them?'

Palmer nodded in agreement. 'Well we shall just have to go back and find out which girl it was that fell out of the window.'

'No, hang on.' Gheeta hit a different programme. 'Miss Jacobs, the accounts lady, said that the Coroner gave a verdict of Accidental Death on that.'

'So?'

'Coroner's Court records will have all the information.' She tapped excitedly on her keyboard as

Claire and Palmer watched. 'For that area and that year it came under the Camberwell Coroner's Court.' More tapping. 'Nineteen eighty four……..blimey there are hundreds of verdicts here….busy court…..let's try Accidental Death….can't have been too many of them……eight……have to read them individually to find our girl.'

Palmer had been down this road with Sergeant Singh's bespoke computer programmes before. He gave a little cough into his hand. 'Ahem, I take it that logging into a Coroner's Court Archive is totally legal Sergeant?'

Claire tried to conceal a large smile.

Gheeta winked at her as she answered. Both Palmer and Claire knew what was coming. 'I couldn't possibly comment Sir.'

'Mmmm…because I couldn't possibly sanction illegal hacking were it to be brought to my attention, however were it not to be brought to my attention then I wouldn't know about it would I,' he said. It was a statement not a question.

'No sir, you wouldn't……..and her name was Angela Bennett. Nineteen years old doing a Combined Arts Course….I suppose that's a bit of everything. Enrolled January 1984 and death occurred on September 19th…..Parents attended the court on October 4th as did the pathologist and …..this is interesting…..the parents questioned the courts findings and the verdict.'

Claire had been busy on her PC and spoke up. 'Hang on a tick.' She worked away. 'Right, I've got the local newspaper, South London Press for the day after the court hearing, October 5th, and they ran a story and a picture of the parents outside the court look.' She pulled it up onto her screen as Palmer bent to read it.

A minute later he stood upright. 'Better print that off for us please Claire. It seems the parents thought their daughter's death was suicide caused by continual bullying at the College.' He sat down and folded his arms. 'Interesting, very interesting. So we could have a parent or parents getting revenge on those who they blamed for their daughters bullying and suicide?' He thought for a moment before continuing. 'Or we could have young Angela Bennett being the first victim of our current killer who is starting up again from where he or she left off in nineteen eighty four after a long hiatus?'

'So where do we go from here Sir?' Gheeta could see quite a few avenues of investigation opening up but which one was the key?

'Well,' Palmer stroked his chin, 'that's a difficult choice.' He pondered a few moments more. 'Right, first I think we pull the teams back in and trace all the class of nineteen eighty four that are still around. They all have to be warned not to stay in any hotel, and they all have to be interviewed, nice and easily, to see if we can get a handle on this bullying claim the parents made. Who was doing it and to who. With a bit of luck we'll find out that our three victims were the bullies and revenge has been taken by Angela Bennett's dad if he's still alive. On the other hand, if the bullies had more victims it could be any one of them from nineteen eighty four having her revenge on them.'

'So every girl from the class of nineteen eighty four could be a potential victim or a potential killer then?' Gheeta could see a problem with interviewing them without warning off the killer if she was actually one of them or frightening the rest of the class without cause.

Palmer nodded. 'This one will have to be done very 'softly, softly'. Priority is to safeguard *Friday's Child* and *Saturday's child* whoever they might be.'

Claire added. '*Friday's Child is loving and giving, Saturday's child works hard for a living.* Don't sound like labels to hang on bullies. Just about everybody could claim to be either of those.'

Gheeta nodded. 'It's not going to be easy to pin either of those labels on just one of the class Sir.'

'No, no it's not is it. Try asking them all for the names of those who were bullied *and* the bullies. Can't think that a bully is going to own up even now but we might get a couple of recurring names. Meanwhile get an update on the Bennetts and where they live. That is if they are still alive. They've got to be number one suspects should the information we get from the girls of the class point to suicide because of this bullying.'

Chapter 17

It wasn't an easy job tracing the *class of 1984*. The team were brought back to the Yard and split into pairs before being sent out to find the girls of *class of 1984* and tread very lightly with interviews, the aim of which was to really get into the make-up of the class and who was doing what. Who the bullies were, who were their victims. It had occurred to Palmer that bullies he'd known usually have that trait ingrained in their make-up and once a bully always a bully so in all probability there had been more than one victim. Which could of course mean that there may well be more than one girl who had bided her time and was now out for revenge. As the saying goes, it's a meal best served cold.

None of the present staff at the College were employed there at that time except Timms-Beddis and those that were had passed away or were now so infirm as to have little memory of the College let alone the *class of 1984*.

It was now a matter of waiting for the team to do the basic ground work, ask the questions and hopefully ring a few bells in the ex student's minds.

Two days later came the breakthrough Palmer was hoping for. Gheeta announced her arrival into the office with a triumphant imitation of a trumpet fanfare.

'Da-d-d-daaaaaaaaa!' she placed a large photo in front of Palmer, 'our little clan of bullies!'

The photo showed all four victims plus two others. 'The one on the right is Angela and next to her is *Friday's Child* the others are the known victims.'

'How do you know that? How do you know she is *Friday's child*?'

'Because the girl who had this photo, now a fifty eight year old check out girl at Morrisons Supermarket gave it to us and named them all.'

'Check out girl at Morrisons? Not exactly the career path she and her parents had hoped for when enrolling in the Milner's College of Dramatic Art.'

'And you won't believe this, the real reason for the nursery rhyme link is not what we thought.'

'Go on.'

'Those girls in this photo put on a self penned small end of term play featuring the poem where each of them played a '*Child*' character. So the killer is using their part in the play to nominate the day he or she kills them.'

'Is this check-out lady at Morrisons *Friday's Child* then? Is that why she kept the photo?'

'No she's not and she can't remember the name of the girl who was so I've got Claire copying this photo out to the team on the mobiles so they can show it to the rest of the class that we've found so far when they interview them and hopefully somebody will come up with a name, or indeed it may be one of them.'

'I hope so.' He thought for a moment. 'Mind you she might just as well be *Saturday's Child*. We don't actually know for definite which day's child is which out of Angela and this other girl do we? Angela could have been Friday and the other girl Saturday?'

'Angela's parents might remember guv?'

'Okay, get Claire to concentrate of finding an address for them. See if they are still in the land of the living.'

Chapter 18

Mr and Mrs Bennett were very much still in the land of the living and still in the council house that Mrs Thatcher had sold them in the 1980's. A well kept, if small, front garden led to the double glazed front door. Palmer pressed the bell and gave Sergeant Singh a look that said 'I'm not looking forward to this.'

Mister Bennett answered the door. He was rather frail and in his late seventies walking with the aid of a stick. He greeted them warmly. Gheeta had rung ahead and told him they would be coming to chat informally about the College. She had purposely avoiding mentioning his daughter's death although it was pretty obvious that would be the subject. There didn't seem to be a Mrs Bennett around as ushered them into the lounge and they made themselves comfortable on the on the large sofa. They declined the offer of tea and biscuits.

'Well Chief Superintendent this sounds all very mysterious. Has it anything to do with Angela? I suppose it must have. No other reason why you should be here to talk about the College. It seems so long ago now although I think of her every day.'

Palmer felt so sad for this elderly gentleman who had carried such grief for so long. 'I'm sure you do Mister Bennett, I'm sure you do. Unfortunately it does concern her in a small way.' He tried to ease the old chap's worry as best he could. 'You see we have had a couple of rather nasty crimes committed against some of the other girls that were in Angela's year and amongst her circle of friends. Although now of course they are not girls anymore, all grown up middle aged ladies.'

'Her circle of friends,' Bennett smiled ruefully. 'She didn't have many friends at that awful place. I take it you are familiar with the events surrounding her suicide?'

Palmer and Gheeta noted his use of the word.

'Indeed we are Sir, which is why we are here as you rightly assumed. You see from our enquiries it would seem that Angela may not have been the only one that suffered bullying at the College at that time and we are trying to get a picture of it all. I'd like to show you a picture of some of the girls including your daughter if it won't upset you too much? Just to see if you can recognise any of them even after all this time. Would you mind taking a look?'

'Don't worry it won't upset me at all.' He pointed to picture of his daughter on a sideboard, 'I have a chat with her every day.'

Palmer smiled and handed him the photo of the six girls. He took a while looking at it.

'Bastards all of them,' there was no malice in his voice, his anger had abated over the years but his heart hadn't forgiven. 'These creatures were the cause of my daughter's suicide a little band of bullying bastards. And they all got away with it.'

'Until now Sir.' Palmer took the photo back.

'What, what do you mean until now'? Is that stupid Coroner's verdict being quashed at long last?'

'No Sir, but the nasty crimes that I said are being committed against some of the girls now, are being committed against those girls in that photo. They are being murdered one by one.'

Mister Bennett was silent. He didn't seem surprised. Palmer didn't want to break the silence he wanted to hear Bennett's next sentence. It was important.

Bennett looked him straight in the eye. 'Good.'

Palmer kept silent.

'Good good good. I knew that Angela wouldn't be the only one. I knew there were other bullied girls in that year who were too scared of those bastards to speak up. Good, bloody good. Hope they all suffered. We certainly have.'

'Did Angela have any good friends at all at the college Sir, any one single close friend maybe that she would confide in?'

'No she wasn't there long enough really.' A light turned on in Bennett's mind. 'Looking for a revenge motive are you Chief Superintendent? You're probably on the right track too. Could be anybody effected by those shits.' He looked up at Sergeant Singh. 'Please excuse my language dear but if I were able and had the opportunity I'd probably take great joy in killing them myself.' He paused for a moment as a thought hit him. 'Do you suspect me?'

Gheeta smiled. 'I don't think so Sir.'

Mister Bennett laughed quietly. 'No, not with two replacement knees and I still need my hips done. An old man walking with sticks would stand out a bit.'

'Is Mrs Bennett around Sir?' Palmer needed to ask.

Bennett laughed again. 'Oh my, I don't think you have a suspect there, she's been in a care home with dementia for five years.'

'Oh I am so sorry Sir, we didn't know that. You'll forgive us if we check that though just to tick all the boxes.'

'Of course I'll give you the details.'

Chapter 19

Gheeta clicked off from her mobile and turned to Palmer as they travelled in the squad car back to the yard.

'It checks out guv they've had Mrs Bennett in the home for over five years and on the very rare occasions she goes out it's always with a nurse. She has Severe Dementia.'

'So it's going to be one of the college girls then.' Palmer relaxed in the back of the car at least they were cutting down the number of suspects by two

Gheeta nodded from the front passenger seat. 'Looks like it, or if there were other victims of the bullying, it could well be a relative of one of them.'

'We need to find that other girl in the picture.' He straightened his right leg out as a twinge of sciatica raked it. 'She's the only one left alive of the bullies and she can't possibly know what danger she's in.'

'So where do we start to look for the killer now Sir?'

Palmer exhaled loudly. 'God only knows Sergeant, God only knows. We just keep interviewing and asking questions and hope one name comes up a few times for another bullied girl. Can't see anybody else taking revenge on those women except somebody they tormented.'

Chapter 20

Steak and kidney pie in the microwave, four minutes.
So read the note Mrs P had left for Palmer. He'd
forgotten it was her Gardening Club night and she
was off down to the local community hall to discuss
fuchsia cuttings and tomato blight with the other fans
of Monty Don who gathered there once a month.
Palmer checked his watch, just gone eight. That gave
him a couple of hours grace to eat his meal and laze
about a bit before she returned. Daisy the dog was
alert. She'd seen the steak and kidney pie and was her
master to leave even a smear of gravy on the plate
she'd make a nuisance of herself by his side knowing
that he'd eventually put it down for her. Something
Mrs P would never do. Palmer smiled at Daisy and
gave her a pat. 'You crafty bitch, you think you're
going to get some eh?' He took the plate from the
microwave placed it on a tray with a glass of cider
from the fridge and he and the dog wandered into the
lounge to switch on Sky and catch the midweek
match.

How he managed not to drop the tray and end up
with steak and kidney all over the carpet is a miracle.

'What the…..!!'

The television was already on and beaming from the
forty inch plasma screen was the unmistakeable fake
tanned face of Benji.

It spoke. 'Hello Justin, how are you, had a good
day?'

'What the….what are you doing on my telly?'

'I'm on Skype. Your good lady and I set it all up yesterday. We had a little chat earlier about roses before she went off to her club and she must have left it on. Good isn't it, especially with a large family like yours. That looks nice what have you got?'

'Got?'

'On the tray, your meal looks appetising.'

'Can you see me?'

'Of course I can that's what Skype is for. We put a webcam on top of your set.'

Palmer noticed the small lens peeping at him from a black plastic holder sitting on the set. He wasn't having this. He put his tray down on the sofa, crossed to the set, took the webcam and turned it face down on the television table.

'Goodnight Benji.'

'Wait a minute Justin, I'll tell you how to shut the programme down properly.......'

'I know how to do that thank you Benji, goodnight.' He flicked the remote to the football channel and spoke to Daisy. 'That's quite enough of that. Having Benji next door is bad enough without having him in the ruddy lounge!'

'I heard that.'

'Are you still there?'

'The program's still running so I can still hear you. I'll said I'd tell you how to shut it down properly, you have to close the programme not just switch channels.'

Palmer lent behind the set and pulled the plug from the wall socket. 'That settles that.'

He turned back to the sofa where Daisy lay licking her lips and looking very contented next to an empty plate on his tray.

Chapter 21

Marion Stanley was tired. It had been a busy day and she was tired. Having just got in to her Lincoln home and poured a much needed glass of red wine from the fridge in her kitchen all she wanted was some peace and quiet and now the damn phone was ringing. She answered it in a fed up manner.

'Hello?'

'Hello is that Marion Stanley?' asked the female voice on the other end.

'It is.'

'Hello Mrs Stanley it's the Guardian newspaper Arts section.'

'Oh yes?' Her manner changed to very bright and businesslike. What the Devil could they want with her?

'Mrs Stanley will you be going to the London Literary Review Conference as we'd like to get an interview with you about the problems of being an 'out of town' agent?'

Marion laughed. 'Yes I'm going up for the Conference. No problems being an 'out of town' agent, as you put it, you just have to work ten times as hard as your London rivals.' She laughed.

'Oh I'm sure there is much more to it than that Mrs Stanley. Would you be prepared to give us some of your time? It shouldn't take too long'

Being an 'out of town' Literary Agent, Marion Stanley was adept at seizing every opportunity to get publicity for her stable of authors and this sounded like an opportunity not to be missed. The Conference was an annual get together where agents could overstate the quality of their authors and badger publishers into deals. A name piece in any newspaper's Arts section would be good but in the Guardian, well respected for its Arts coverage, it would be excellent a real coup.

'Yes of course I will I'm there from next Thursday through to the following Monday.'

'That's fine probably be the Friday. We can make it after the daytime Conference session so as to intrude as little as possible on your business time. Plus if we can do it on the Friday we can get it into the Sunday Arts supplement. Would an hour or so at your hotel Friday evening suit you?'

'Perfect, I'm at the Carlton Towers, Edgware road.'

'I know it. So if we have somebody come round about seven in the evening how does that sound?'

'Yes that sounds good, I'll look forward to it. Thank you.'

'No, thank you, I'm sure it will make a very interesting piece, seven on Friday it is then, thank you so much. Have a good Conference. Goodbye.'

'I will. Goodbye and thank you.' She put the phone on its hook and finished off the rest of her glass of wine as her husband came in from the garden with a bunch of freshly picked sweet peas.

'Hello dear,' he said and gave her peck on cheek. 'Had a good day?'

'It just got better. That was the Guardian newspaper on the phone. They want to do an interview with me at the Conference about being an agent outside the London bubble.'

'The Guardian, my word how nice,' he started to strip leaves off the pea stalks. 'Sweet peas are really good this year.'

'Stick them up your arse.'

'Pardon dear?' He was used to her abuse so just carried on stripping the stems.

Marion Stanley could have retired early when her husband retired but her vanity and egoistic selfishness of being *'in the publishing business'* had won the day.

'I work my fingers to the bone whilst you piss about in the garden all day. I get an opportunity like this from a National paper and all you can say is *'the fucking peas are good this year'*.' She poured another glass of wine and went through to the lounge where she spread out on the large sofa and started to think of how she could use the upcoming interview to her financial advantage.

If the truth be known Marion Stanley was a disappointment. Not to anybody else but herself. Always arrogant and selfish and being an 'only child' of wealthy parents she had wanted for nothing. The pony, the clothes, the Milner College acting course where everybody except Marion Stanley could see that she had very little talent. After college she had tried to create herself an acting career with various third rate agents and was kept afloat by her parents money and topless shoots for foreign magazines done on the quiet. Then her parents saw the light and the 'get a proper job' ultimatum was given. The proper job was in a Literary Agents office dealing with various celebrity autobiographies, ghosted and otherwise, and that led her into contact with publishing houses and the feeling she could do a better job promoting authors than the company she worked for.

So she took the plunge and went out alone. She was moderately successful by running her business along vanity publishing lines. She soon realised that many aspiring authors would pay for her services to publish, promote and get their book or books into reviewers' hands and onto bookshop shelves. In Marion Stanley's case they paid a hundred percent of the costs plus her charges. Yes, she felt good it would be nice to have a piece in one of the better Sunday Art Supplements. Perhaps a few of the publisher's that never returned her calls might then start to do so.

Chapter 22

Palmer survived Mrs P's blast of rebuke when he got home the next evening after Benji had told her of their Skype encounter.

'Well fancy leaving it on, I could have wandered into the lounge in my underpants!'

'Oh? And since when do you wander around this house in your underpants Justin Palmer, certainly not when I'm at home!'

'Okay, well not my pants as such but I might have had a shower and just had a towel on or my dressing gown flapping about. Last thing I want to come home to is bloody Benji in the lounge!'

'No need to swear. And how could you tell him it's bad enough having him living next door let alone on the telly. That was a nasty thing to say!'

'I thought I'd turned the set off. I didn't say it for him to hear.'

'Well he did hear it and he was very upset. All the things he's done for us.'

'Only thing I recall him doing for us is flooding your rose garden when his hot tub split.' Palmer smiled at the memory.

Chapter 23

It was the following Wednesday. Palmer's team were working all hours tracing and interviewing the Milner College students from the class of 1984. Many did recall a little clique of bullies who picked on the weakest, but names were not remembered and most just put the bullying down to the usual pecking order of school and college life. *Friday's Child* was obviously not in possession of a strikingly memorable personality that had stuck with her contemporaries. Nobody could name her positively.

Claire interrupted Palmer and Gheeta's review of the evidence, what little there was of it. She had a smile on her face. 'It's not a breakthrough Sir but one name has come up three times on the photo recognition of *Friday's Child*. Three of girls from the year think she was a Marilyn or Marion. No surname.'

'It's a start.' Palmer was pleased.

'And the college roll lists three Marilyns and two Marions in that year,' she added and passed the list to Gheeta. 'That's all of them and their known addresses at the time.'

Gheeta gave it quick look. 'Right, let's go and check if our teams have interviewed any of them already.' She left with Claire to use the landlines in the Team Room leaving the direct lines to Palmer's office open, just in case.

She was back in twenty minutes. 'All cleared except one Sir. Marion Tolley last known address was in Grantham, Lincolnshire. The team did a visit last week and drew a blank. The Tolley family were not

known. We've done a search of the Local Council
Rates List archives and they do list a Bernard Tolley
being resident in 1984 but moved out in nineteen
ninety two. Claire's trying to do a nationwide trace
on him now. Fingers crossed he's *Friday Child's*
parent and can lead us to her.'

'And lead us to her before our killer finds her.'
Palmer looked down at the photo on his desk, 'if she
is *Friday's Child.*'

Chapter 24

The trace on Mr Tolley took a few hours due to his being a middle management Bank official and his Bank had moved him around the branches at regional level during his working life. He had then retired to Hayle in Cornwall and was enjoying a well deserved final salary supported retirement with his wife. The visit by plain clothes police from Palmer's team was out of his comfort zone. *So many dodgy bank operations around the time he was a manager had been brought to light lately, Payment Protection Insurance scam, Libor and interest rate fixing so his immediate thought was that he'd somehow been involved in one without knowing it. But the questions didn't relate to his career at all. Which was a relief but why did the police want to know where his daughter Marion was living now? They were very secretive but it was obviously something important. And why did they ask if Marion was the same Marion Tolley who attended Milner College all those years ago? Yes she was. And the picture they showed him was of Marion and some of her friends from way back when she was at that College. What a waste of money that had been. He remembered the rows he had with his wife about sending Marion there. She was a spoilt child, a single child and a petulant child. If he'd had his way she would have been packed off to boarding school to learn something of use not some arty farty college just because she wanted to be an actress. Waste of time and money. Plus all the financial support afterwards renting a London flat and giving her an allowance. Then there was the 'publishing' business. That would have gone under without Marion's husband's support on the financial side. Her husband was a secure civil servant in Local Government so pretty bomb proof in his job and if they did want to make him redundant it would have been a large severance package and an equally large pension to follow. Mr Tolley was convinced then and now that marriage was one of convenience for Marion. His wife had flown into a rage when he used the term 'gold digger' to describe their daughter's rather surprising and quick marriage. But he'd never seen any real affection between them and she treated her husband like dirt even when company was present. However the publishing business seemed to go well after a few years and then when Marion became financially secure mum and dad were just about forgotten. Shunted into a siding to be phoned on birthdays and Christmas. God knows how that husband of hers puts up with it. But what the Devil has she done to have the police looking for her?* He'd given them her address and now he and his wife had the company of a uniformed WPC for the rest of the day at least. *What would the neighbours think?*

Chapter 25

It was a nice house on the outskirts of Lincoln. Detached modern in Georgian style with a well kept front garden a short tarmac drive to an integral garage and a canopied front door. Palmer quite liked it but not Lincolnshire, too flat and windy. Where had all the forests where Robin Hood had once hid gone eh? All ploughed up for root vegetables by the look of it. On the journey up he'd noticed the vast fields of leek and carrot crops all in precise lines broken now and then by a small gang of immigrant pickers following a tractor throwing the produce into its trailer as they bent against the wind to gather in the harvest. His mind wandered to the Harvest Festivals they had at school when he was a kid in SE24 attending St Saviours Church School. How mum had loaded him down with fruit and vegetables to place on the Chancel steps as the vicar beamed down at him. And how Howard Hudson always only gave a tin of beans and nobody ever said a word because his dad was a copper.

He pushed the bell. 'Fingers crossed she's in.'

'No car in the drive guv and the garage is empty.' Gheeta wasn't hopeful.

They'd had a plain squad car from the local force sit outside since Mr Tolley had given them his daughter's address. No phone contact had been made as Palmer didn't want Marion Stanley, her married name, to behave in anyway but normal.

The report from the squad car was that nothing had come and nothing had left. Palmer tried to banish the thought that the killer had beaten them to the house and inside he might find......his thoughts were broken as the door opened and Mr Stanley's welcoming smile soon faded when he saw Palmer flourishing a warrant card and Gheeta and a local officer both in uniform.

'Mr Stanley?' Palmer smiled as he asked.

'Oh my God. What's happened? Has she had an accident?' The colour drained from his face.

'Nobody has had an accident as far as we are aware Sir. Is Mrs Stanley at home?'

'No, no she's away on business. What's this about?'

'May we come in?' Palmer didn't wait for an answer and stepped inside into the hall. 'There are a few questions we'd like to ask you Sir. Don't worry it's just information. Is there somewhere we could go?'

Mr Stanley had regained a little composure. 'Yes, yes of course. Come through into the lounge.' He led him down the hall and into a large lounge with a conservatoire leading off French doors. Gheeta followed and the uniform officer waited at the front door quietly closing it. 'Sit down, please sit down.' Mr Stanley waved at a sofa and arm chairs. 'What on earth is all this about?' His facial expression went from disbelief to acute worry and back to disbelief as Palmer explained the situation in full.

'Well Marion's always been a bit feisty but I wouldn't have thought she was the bullying type,' he lied knowing full well that his wife was a prime candidate for that label.

'Does she have a mobile Sir?' Gheeta asked.

'She does yes, but it's usually turned off when she goes away on business.'

'And where has she gone away to Sir?' Palmer smiled benignly realising that he had to treat this chap with kid gloves.

'She's at the London Literary Review Conference…..she's a Literary Agent, looks after authors and that sort of thing, it's at the South Bank Conference Centre in London.'

'Would you like to try her mobile Sir, just in case it's on?'

'Oh yes, of course, yes, yes.' He crossed to where a telephone sat on a side table and flicked through the diary beside it. 'I Never can remember phone numbers…..especially the mobile ones, so many digits….ah here we are.' He dialled out as Palmer and Gheeta waited hopefully. 'No answer, I didn't think there would be.'

'Okay,' Palmer nodded to Gheeta. 'See what you can do Sergeant.' He knew full well that by fair means or foul Gheeta would find out where Marion Stanley was.

'Do you have the internet in here Sir?' Gheeta asked.

'Yes, my wife spends an awful lot of time on it.'

'And WiFi?'

'WiFi?' Stanley was pretty ignorant on such things.

Gheeta explained. 'A wireless connection to the internet, no cables and plugs?'

'Errrrr, no, no I don't think so no cables. Marion sometimes uses her laptop in the garden though.'

'Then you have got WiFi Sir…okay, not a problem.' She gave him a smile.

Opening her laptop and plugging in her mobile to the laptop USB to get a WiFi signal she went to work as Palmer stood and peered through the French doors to the immaculate garden. Not a weed to be seen. This chap and Mrs P would get on like a house on fire.

Mister Stanley sat watching Sergeant Singh chasing his wife's whereabouts. Google told her the contact numbers for the London Literary Review organisers and two calls later, as Palmer was once again assuring a worried Mister Stanley that his wife was probably safe and sound, she was speaking to the Delegate's List Secretary who gave her the four most likely hotels that Marion Stanley would have booked into and promised to have her name put on the reception desk 'message waiting' notice board.

'Right then we'll leave you in peace Sir and go and find your wife.' Palmer walked to the door. 'If she does contact you please don't alarm her and do give her our phone number if you would.'

He nodded to Gheeta who fetched a card from her shoulder bag pocket and gave it to him as Palmer continued. 'There's a plain squad car from your local police station outside and the chaps will be keeping a presence here until this matter is all over. So rest assured your safety is being taken care of. You've nothing to worry about Sir.'

No nothing to worry about thought Gheeta as they bade their goodbyes and made their way out, just a serial killer on the loose who has murdered three women and has your wife down as the next target. Other than that nothing to worry about Sir, have a nice day.

Chapter 26

It was early evening. The gentle knock on Marion
Stanley's hotel room door was barely audible above
the sound of her hot bath running in the adjacent bath
room. She hadn't ordered any room service. She
straightened the complimentary hotel bath robe she
was wearing and squinted through the security peep
hole. She could see a lady clasping a shoulder bag.

'Who is it?' Marion asked loudly.

'I'm from the Guardian Arts section to see Marion
Stanley. My editor has arranged for an interview with
her?'

'Oh….err oh yes. Give me one minute please.' She
hurried to the bathroom and turned off the tap, tidied
the scattered papers and note books on the table and
bed, puffed up her hair and opened the door.

'I'm Marion Stanley.' They shook hands. 'Please
excuse the bath robe…I was just going to take a long
hot soak. Do come in I wasn't expecting you just yet.
I expected a call first.'

'Oh I'm sorry…yes I should have rung first really
but so many people to see and the editor wanted your
interview for this Sunday which means I have to get it
to the layout chaps early tomorrow morning.'

She was older than Marion had imagined the general
run of reporters to be. Well into her sixties at a guess
but well groomed in a grey trouser suit and with no
attempt to colour away the grey hair tied neatly in a
bun at the back of her head. Frameless spectacles and
a lack of make up completed the picture.

'I've done some research already so it shouldn't take up too much of your time.'

'Do sit down please Miss? Mrs......?' Marion Stanley indicated the one guest chair provided by the hotel and sat on the edge of the bed herself.

'Bennett, Mrs Bennett. Thank you,' she said and sat in the chair and opened her file. 'I was amazed to see that you went to the Milner College of Dramatic Art.'

'Yes, I did.' Marion gave a little laugh. 'I had illusions of grandeur in those days. Of setting the theatrical world alight with my talent. Total waste of time of course but why were you amazed that I went there?'

'My daughter went there at the same time as you.'

'No really? There's a coincidence.' Marion thought that might bode well for a decent write-up. 'What was her name I might have known her?'

'I've a picture actually.' Bennett pulled a large photo from her shoulder bag. The same one as Palmer had got from the Morrison's checkout lady. She stood and crossed to stand beside Marion Stanley holding the bag and gave her the photo. 'That's my daughter Angela Bennett, she's the one on the far right.' Her voice was hard. 'Oh you knew her alright. You're second from the right. Do you recognise them all? You were all in a play based on the poem *Monday's Child*. Do you remember that? You're the only one left now.'

Marion Stanley didn't understand and was a bit worried the way the conversation was going. 'The only one left?'

'The others are all dead.'

This wasn't the sort of interview Marion Stanley had had in mind. She was feeling very uncomfortable. The figure of this woman standing over her was becoming threatening. 'Dead, all of them dead, I don't understand. What has this to do with my interview?

'Nothing, absolutely nothing, you see Angela,' Bennett pointed to the far right girl in the photo, 'my daughter, committed suicide after being horribly bullied, bullied by you and those others.'

'I don't…I can't…' Marion was struggling to make sense of the situation she was in.

'So I've taken revenge for my daughter and killed them all and now it's your turn.'

From the corner of her eye Marion Stanley saw Bennett's bag fall to the floor revealing that she was holding a large carving knife which flashed in the light as it was plunged into her throat.

Pulling the knife back Bennett stepped away from the bed as Marion Stanley slid slowly off it to the floor wide eyed and gurgling, clutching her throat as life slowly ebbed from her body with the growing stream of blood soaking her bathrobe.

Bennett turned and went calmly into the bathroom, plunged the knife into the waiting bath of hot water to clean it, pulled out the bath plug and after wiping the knife on a towel retrieved her shoulder bag and photo, then placing a small piece of paper with the word *'Friday's Child'* written on it onto the bed she left the room. She felt an overwhelming feeling of elation, of freedom, and smiled broadly to her reflection in the lift's mirrored wall as it descended to the ground floor. As she walked through the crowded lobby on her way out she didn't notice the two plain clothes policemen at the reception desk asking whether a 'Marion Stanley' was booked in?

Chapter 27

Palmer and Sergeant Singh arrived at the Carlton Tower Hotel as fast as possible after being alerted on their car radio by the Officers who had established that Marion Stanley was the occupant of a room but they got no reply to their knocking and had got the hotel manager to open the door revealing the bloody scene inside just a minute before Palmer arrived. Mrs Stanley was still gurgling slightly as he and Singh came into the room, and the hotel doctor was vainly trying to save her. It was not to be and she died with a last, long gurgle. The doctor stood up.

'Sorry Chief Superintendent she's gone. Not a lot I could do the wind pipe was almost completely severed. That cut was made with some force.'

Palmer nodded. He wasn't a squeamish type but the sight of an almost decapitated Mrs Stanley was not pleasant, 'Thank you Doctor I appreciate your efforts.'

The Doctor nodded and made to wash his bloodied hands in the bathroom. Gheeta blocked him.

'Sorry Doctor, could I ask you wash up somewhere else please? It's a crime scene now. Quite a serious one and the killer may have used the bathroom.'

'Of course,' he said and looked enquiringly at the manager, 'Charles do you have an empty room on the floor where I could.......?' He waved his hands at the manager who seemed to be transfixed with the awful scene in the room.

'What?...oh, yes of course come along I'll open one up.' They left together.

'I see we have the note left again Sir.' Gheeta bent over the body.

'Mmmmmm,' Palmer was thinking, 'probably be as much use as the other notes. I'll tell you what Sergeant go down to reception and see if there's any CCTV we can see. For once we are right on the ball here she's been killed in the last hour so people's memories will be fresh too. Have a word with the staff on duty and see if they can remember anybody asking for Mrs Stanley's room number.'

'Right guv.' As she left the local West End Central forensics team started to arrive as did the photographer and pathologist. Time to leave thought Palmer and after giving them a briefing he made his way down to catch up with Gheeta who was taking short statements from the staff.

'Anything?'

'Nothing yet Sir, they've been quite busy with this Literary Conference going on. Lots of new faces but nobody causing any concern, one thing though…'

'Yes?'

'Whoever went to Mrs Stanley's room new the room number. None of the reception staff recall anybody asking for her room number and if anybody had they wouldn't have given it. Hotel policy, they'd find out who the person was and ring Mrs Stanley on the internal phone to see if it was okay to give it.'

'It could have been somebody from the Conference who she'd given the number to.'

'No, she didn't check in until this evening after the Conference ended for the day. She wouldn't have known the room number.'

'Interesting…….any CCTV?'

'Yes but only in the reception area, no cameras on the floors.'

'That's disappointing. Get a copy made and sent to Claire'

The Manager and Hotel Doctor came out of the lift and across to them.

'One thing I forgot to tell you Chief Superintendent.' The doctor was almost apologetic.

'Yes?'

'Mrs Stanley was just about alive when I got to her at first, and she was trying to say something. It was very mumbled as you can imagine with such an injury and I was intent on working to save her and not really listening, but it sounded like 'Benny' Can't be sure but she repeated it a few times before she left us.'

'Benny?' Palmer repeated it back.

'Yes or something similar.'

Palmer turned to Gheeta. 'Are you thinking what I'm thinking Sergeant?'

She nodded. 'Bennett.'

'Couldn't be could it? He's old and can hardly walk and his wife's in a care home.' He turned to the Doctor. 'Thank you Doctor, we may have to take a statement at a later date if that's all right?'

'Of course, well, I am afraid I have to go. Sorry to have met you both in such awful circumstances. I hope you get the killer quickly. These people can acquire a taste for it if they get away with one.'

The manager put him right. 'The Chief Superintendent is head of the *Serial* Murder Squad at Scotland Yard.'

'Oh, sorry,' the doctor was a little embarrassed, 'sort of teaching my granny to suck eggs then, apologies

Chief Superintendent.' He shook Palmer's hand and was gone.

Palmer turned back to Gheeta. 'We didn't physically check on Mrs Bennett did we? Perhaps her dementia is not as bad as they think, could be a smoke screen. Get on the phone to the Care Home and ask that somebody checks on her whereabouts right now. I want to know that she's in her room now or at least in the Home now. And then check with the surveillance unit at Mr Bennett's house and see what he's been up to. Has he been out at all today, I know he said he's got dodgy knees and a stick to walk with but I've seen those benefit cheats on television shows, staggering around on sticks all week and playing rugby at the weekends!'

Sergeant Singh moved off to a quiet corner of the lobby to make the calls as Palmer sat and started to turn the case over again in his mind. What had they missed? If Mrs Bennett was in the Home and Mr Bennett in his….who the hell was the 'Bennett' that Marion Stanley had gurgled out? Angela hadn't any siblings, no brothers or sisters and Claire's digging into the family had not come up with any close relatives, uncles, aunts, cousins or the like. Was he on the completely wrong track? Maybe the killer was unconnected with the Bennetts but knew about their loss and was using it as a smoke screen, a red herring? A crafty psychopath who'd used them as a cover to kill? And a damn crafty psychopath if he or she was.

Gheeta returned carrying a coffee for each of them.

'Compliments of the Hotel guv,' she said and sat opposite him. 'Mrs Bennett is in the lounge at the

Home as we speak and Mr Bennett is indoors and has not been out all day.'

Another dead end.

'We are missing something Sergeant, God knows what but there's a link somewhere. The killer knew who the bullies were, knew about Angela Bennett's suicide and was enough of a friend to take revenge for her.'

Gheeta was puzzled. 'But why wait so long for revenge guv?'

'I don't know perhaps the need for revenge has been growing inside our killer over the years and becoming more and more important in his or her warped little mind as time marches on gradually taking over their thoughts and life until it becomes an obsession and has to be done? Like a tumour that has to be removed at some point.'

'Yuk…,' Gheeta grimaced, 'there must be a relative we've missed. Both Claire and I have scoured the Births and Deaths registers and I'm positive there's nobody related to Angela or her parents we haven't found. I'll go back through it all again in the morning.'

Palmer finished his coffee and stood up. 'Oh well, no more we can do tonight. I've told forensics that if they come up with anything to ring me at home but I don't think they'll find anything. They haven't at the other murder scenes so we might actually get an early night Sergeant.' He put on his trilby. 'At least there are no more *'childs'* to worry about. The only worry is that now the killer has finished his or her list she or he will just disappear.'

'Or start another list guv?'

Chapter 28

Getting home by nine-o-clock was not an often enjoyed bonus for Palmer when a case was ongoing. He had thought about going back to his office at the Yard and wading through the case files again in the hope that something that they'd missed so far would jump out. But he had been through them countless times already and the thought of an early night with the added treat of a Barcelona La Liga game being live on Sky Sports was too much. So he was a bit peeved when he entered the house, hung his coat and Prince of Wales jacket on the hallstand, perched his trilby on top of it and gave Daisy the dog a good 'hello' cuddle only to hear voices from the lounge.

Mrs P's Garden Club meet was next week and she hadn't said that any of the famil were coming over. Not that that made any difference as they seemed to drop in all the time, usually just as he settled on the sofa with a good book or when 'Barca' had just kicked off.

'Only me,' he shouted just in case his arrival hadn't been noticed.

'We are in the lounge Justin,' Mrs P replied.

'Okay.' He took a home-made cheese straw from the biscuit barrel on the kitchen table, a bottle of cider from the fridge, prized off its top and went to join them.

'The *'we'* in the lounge were Mrs P on the sofa and Benji on Skype on the telly.

He gave her a perfunctory kiss and flopped down next to her. 'Can't you turn him off,' he whispered trying not to move his lips, 'big match starts in a couple of minutes.'

'Where's your plate you'll get cheesey crumbs all down the side of the sofa.' Came back the understanding reply.

Palmer thought that, '*Hello dear, nice to have you home early for once and have you had a good day*' would be more the greeting he'd like rather than an admonishment about cheesey crumbs. His mouth was full so he just grunted back.

From the television Benji waved a hand. 'Yoohoo Justin, how are you?'

Palmer nodded back to the TV screen aware of the replaced webcam sittingback on top of it.

'Benji's been telling me how to divide my Azaelias.'

'Barcelona's kicking off in two minutes,' he mumbled to her from the corner of his full mouth.

'You have to make sure your spade's sharp,' was Benji's contribution from the screen.

Palmer cleared his mouth with a gulp of cider from the bottle. 'It's live on Sky.'

Mrs P nudged him with a sharp elbow. 'Where's your glass, Benji will think we've no manners drinking from the bottle.'

Benji was still dividing Azaelias. 'You can always take half ripe cuttings and dip them in a rooting hormone before putting them into a cutting compost over winter. They'll shoot up in the spring.'

'Or you can go and buy some from the Garden Centre down the road,' Palmer couldn't resist it.

Benji was shocked. 'Oh no, no, no, no, that is the lazy way Justin. Not the true gardener's way of doing things at all! Monty Don would never do that!'

'He would if he supported Barcelona.' Palmer put his hand over his mouth as he whispered to Mrs P. 'What's he doing on the telly he only lives next door! You could talk about your blooming Azaelias over the fence.' He checked his watch. 'The match has started now. I've got a monthly standing order to Sky Sports not to Benji's Gardening Tips.'

Benji was in full flow. 'Tomorrow Justin I'm coming round and we're going to replace your strawberry plants so you'll have a fresh and tasty crop in the summer.'

'Nothing wrong with the strawberry plants, last summer's crop was okay.' Palmer remembered just how tasty they had been.

Mrs P was getting a little annoyed at him. 'They were all right yes, but I didn't know that all those runners that grew off the main plants, the ones that *you* threw in the compost bin Justin, should have been kept and the old plants thrown in the compost instead.'

Benji explained. 'You see strawberry plants only last in their prime for three years and then you throw away the old plants and keep the runners to make new plants. The new ones will have bigger and sweeter fruit than the three year old plants. Bit like modern marriages, stick it for a few years and then split up and get new partners.'

'Wish I'd thought of that,' Mrs P's sarcastic whispered aside to Palmer went unheard as his mind raced into overdrive.

'Damn!' He jumped up from the sofa sending cheesey crumbs everywhere in his haste. 'I've got to go, sorry Princess.' He gave a startled Mrs P a quick

kiss and was out into the hall pulling his mobile from
the jacket pocket and ordering a squad car to pick him
up straight away. By the time he'd put his jacket, coat
and trilby back on and got down the drive to the road
it was pulling up the blues full on. He gave the driver
instructions to get to the Yard as quick as possible
and then rang Sergeant Singh to tell her to meet him
there at the office as soon as she could.

Chapter 29

It was eleven at night and in Palmer's team room
Sergeant Singh was tapping the keyboard of the main
computer. Palmer was stood behind her watching
very impatiently shifting from foot to foot.

'If you're right guv we should have noticed this on
the family checks we did.'

'I hope I'm right otherwise I'm in deep trouble with
Mrs P and you've been dragged back here on a wild
goose chase.'

Gheeta smiled to herself. It was not often that
Palmer's hunches didn't bear fruit. She typed away at
the keyboard inputting Bennett's name and known
addresses .The screen scrolled down as it searched
and then up popped a list of Bennett marriages and
divorces. After a few minutes Gheeta smiled.

'It's here guv! Hang on let me come forward a bit
'cause we only downloaded the records up to
Angela's death,' she said as she tapped away, 'these
government data records are so easy to hack into I'm
surprised they aren't played about with by hackers all
the time.'

'Played about with?'

'Yes, I could put in false information, delete stuff
and play havoc if I wanted to. Hang on here we go,
downloading now.' The screen scrolled like a
teleprinter. 'Aha! There it is! The Bennetts got
divorced in nineteen ninety seven and she reverted to
her maiden name of Dorothy Robins …and he, mister
Bennett, remarried in two thousand and one. He
married an Elaine Chard.'

Palmer punched the air. 'Yes! I knew it. So the *Mrs Bennett* confined in the Care Home with dementia is Elaine Chard his second wife. His first wife, and Angela's mother is Dorothy Robins, is she is out and about and probably celebrating the end to a series of murders avenging her daughter's suicide. Benji you're a genius.'

'Benji?' Gheeta knew who Benji was but failed to see any input he might have had into the case.

'Yes, Benji and strawberry plants,' he beamed at Gheeta. 'I'll explain in the morning. Now let's get you a car home. I'm just going to the night room and put out a warrant for Dorothy Robins. I think we need to pay Mister Bennett a visit in the morning. He's a bit of explaining to do.'

Gheeta closed down the computer and put her coat on. 'You think he's playing a part in this guv.?'

'Oh yes, oh yes indeed I do. You don't think his divorce from Angela's mother that he didn't tell us about just slipped his mind do you?'

'No but he seemed like a very nice old man.'

'By all accounts so did Crippen.'

They both laughed as they left the office.

Chapter 30

Mister Bennett watched from behind the net curtains and was not surprised to see Chief Superintendent Palmer and his Detective Sergeant get out of the squad car and walk up his drive. He quite expected them really after the phone call he'd had from Dorothy last night. The same call that he'd had from her after each murder. Just the four words....
'Monday's Child is gone'..... 'Tuesday's Child is gone'..... 'Wednesday's Child is gone'......
'Thursday's Child is gone' and last night, 'Fridays Child is gone'. He walked into the hall and opened the front door before Palmer had time to press the bell.

'Chief Superintendent, this is a surprise.'

'I don't think so Sir.' Palmer barged past him and went into the front room. Sergeant Singh waved an arm to indicate Bennett was to follow, which he did. Once they were all in Palmer rounded on him his voice had a hard edge to it.

'Sit down Mister Bennett.' Bennett did so and Palmer stood over him like a threatening predator. 'At the end of this little chat and dependent on the answers I get from you, I could well be charging you with aiding and abetting a criminal act, withholding evidence, and being an accessory to multiple murders.'

'But I haven't done anything Superintendent?' Bennett feigned amazement.

'Mister Bennett just stop this stupid act of innocence if you would. You told me Mrs Bennett was in a care home and incapable of committing the murders which is very true. What you didn't tell me was that she is the second Mrs Bennett and the first, Dorothy Robins, Angela's birth mother is alive and quite capable of committing murder and so far has probably killed five ladies, killing them all whilst you were protecting her identity from the police by withholding the fact that you had remarried.'

'I told you the truth. You asked where Mrs Bennett was and I told you where Mrs Bennett was. I didn't lie at any time.'

'No, you just forgot the fact that we had been talking about Angela and her class at the Milner College and were asking after Angela's mother did you? The only reason that makes any sense of why you purposely did not tell us about your divorce and remarriage is that you have known all along that Dorothy Robins was out there taking revenge for your daughter's death. You knew we were hunting her and deliberately withheld facts that would help the investigation and help us detain her. I think that the evidence points to you purposely withholding those facts so she could complete her murderous task.'

'I would like a lawyer.'

'Where is she?'

'I would like a lawyer.'

'When did you last have contact with her?'

'I would like a lawyer.'

Palmer gave him an ice cold stare for some time, turned and looked out of the window his back to Bennett. 'And you're going to need one old son. Mister Bennett I am arresting you for wasting Police time, aiding and abetting a criminal act and compliance in a murder or murders. Sergeant cuff him, read him his rights and get him taken to the Yard and held there.'

'But I, I can't just leave here…?'

'You can, why not? Your current wife is in care and now you're in my care. Unfortunately for you I don't think I can offer you the same degree of comfort in the room you're going to spend the next few nights in as that of your current wife's room at the care Home.' He turned back to face Bennett and all but snarled the words out. 'I don't like people like you Mister Bennett.' He walked to the door whilst Sergeant Singh read Bennett his rights and then had one of the uniformed officers take him to the car and off to the Yard.

'You haven't got enough to keep him inside guv you know you haven't,' Gheeta stated the obvious. She knew Palmer would have a reason for taking Bennett into custody on a charge that wouldn't stick. And indeed he had.

'I know that Sergeant but *he* doesn't….well not until the duty Solicitor arrives and goes for bail. And that will take at least a few hours so Mister Bennett will get a taste of what being locked up is like and hopefully the thought of spending the rest of his days like it will loosen his tongue. He knows where Robins is…probably talks to her every day. He knows her plan and he's right on her side. But we can't prove it so we can't hold him on aiding and abetting.'

Having placed a 24 hour uniformed guard on the house Palmer and Singh took another car back to the yard and the office.

Claire knocked and entered his office as soon as she saw them arrive. 'I ran a check on Bennett's phone Sir. He's only got a landline, no mobile registered to him or to that address. Anyway, the interesting thing is that when I ran the murder dates alongside his call archive data it showed that he had a call from the same number on each of the evenings of the murders. A very short call too.'

Gheeta stopped what she was doing. 'What number did the trace come up with?'

'Zilch, It's a pre pay and unregistered. I rang the number but it's been turned off for the last four hours.'

Palmer sat and pushed his chair onto its back legs against the wall as he put his feet up on his desk. 'She's out there somewhere and now her work is done she can bury herself. False name, move about, leave the country. Christ! I forgot that. Sergeant put a 'stop and detain' on Robins at all UK exit points.'

'Yes guv.' Gheeta set about downloading Dorothy Robin's passport details from the Border Security internal data website. In five minutes she'd got the details and flagged up a red alert on Dorothy Robins to all the UK exit points.

Palmer didn't question Gheeta's methods and knew full well that her computer knowledge and expertise had often bypassed the regulatory procedures in a not totally legal way. But he turned a blind eye and didn't ask questions. Even if she'd explained to him how all her 'unauthorised' information from hacked passwords came into them via several proxy servers in East European countries and couldn't be traced back to them, he wouldn't have understood.

'She's not used that passport for twenty years Sir.' Gheeta read out the information.

'Probably not, but she would have had to change it when the divorce came through wouldn't she?'

'She should have, but no amendment or change has been registered.'

Claire had some knowledge on this. 'My mother-in-law remarried and just applied for a new one in her new married name and it came through no problem. Robins might have done that if she'd remarried like Bennett did? Trouble is we don't know her new name if she did remarry.'

Palmer's chair banged back to the floor as he slid his legs off the desk. 'Ouch!' His sciatica gave him a sharp reminder of its presence. 'Good point Claire.' He stood and stretched his leg. 'She may well have remarried and got a totally new name and life. She could even have done the killings without her new husband knowing or even being aware that she'd had a daughter and the way that daughter died.'

Gheeta's internal phone rang. She answered it and listened for a short while. 'Thank you Reg, yes send them through now and I'll let the Chief know.' She put down the receiver and double clenched her fists in the air with joy.

'That was Reg Frome from forensics….'

'They've got a match on some finger prints?' Palmer was racing ahead.

'No.'

'No?'

'No but they have got a video match. They've put all the hotel CCTV recordings from the murder day at each Hotel through a comparison system and in three of them the same lady is seen entering or leaving the hotel.'

'On the day of each murder?'

'Yes'.

'Really?' Palmer could scarcely believe it. 'But when our lads showed the videos to the Hotel Managers they identified everybody as staff or guests and we checked and cleared all the guests.'

'So she must be staff then Sir?'

'Can't be, how could she be a member of staff at three different Hotels? They're not even in the same Hotel Group are they?'

'Reg has emailed a copy of the three videos down now. Let's have a look.'

Claire and Palmer stood behind Gheeta as she opened the file sent from Forensics and ran the video. The three short clips did indeed show the same lady. Smartly dressed and carrying a shoulder bag with her hair neatly tied into a tight bun she looked every inch the executive type.

'She's the right age Sir.' Gheeta observed.

Palmer agreed. 'She is isn't she, but who is she? Right, come on let's get down to the Carlton Tower and get this person identified.'

Chapter 31

'Who?' Palmer and Sergeant Singh were in the Manager's office at the Carlton Tower hotel and had just shown him the video on Sergeant Singh's laptop. He identified the lady immediately.

'Evelyn Dolland.'

'And who is Evelyn Dolland? Is she here now, a staff member?'

'No. She's….'

Gheeta remembered the name and butted in. 'She's the wife of that Security chap Dolland at the murdered Ballerina's hotel sir. They run the agency with the illegal immigrants that Claire dug up. Remember?'

'Central Recruitment,' the manager said, 'that's her company's name. She provides us with catering and housekeeping staff.' He looked worried. 'What's this about illegal immigrants?'

Palmer waved his question aside. 'Nothing, not important. Do you have an address for Central Recruitment?'

The manager took an address book from his desk drawer and thumbed through to the C page. 'Yes here we are, Curzon street, 23 Curzon Street.'

Chapter 32

23 Curzon Street was an Edwardian house converted into offices. Palmer, Singh and two plain clothes officers sat in an unmarked squad car fifty meters down the road from the entrance. Their radio crackled ' Foxtrot two in position Sir. We are in the blue transit ten meters from the target property.'

Foxtrot two was West End Central's Tactical Firearms Unit, or part of it. Four plain clothed armed officers with body armour beneath their jackets. Palmer responded.

'Foxtrot two this is Blue Leader. You've got the picture of the woman we are after. Her name is Evelyn Dolland. She looks like anybody's mum but be very careful she's a history of violence but not armed violence except with knives. Use tasers if threatened as she's nothing to lose if we corner her and I'd like her alive, over.'

'Foxtrot two understood Sir, over'

'Okay in you go in your own time. The office is on the first floor and the name on the door is Central Recruitment. We will follow you in.'

They watched as four burly officers casually stepped from the rear of the transit and meandered along the road in pairs and into number 23. To all intents and purposes just four chaps returning to their office after lunch.

'Right,' Palmer winced as his sciatica caught him unawares when he opened the car door and stood up, 'show time, come on.'

They made their way through the throng of shoppers along the pavement and into number 23. All was quiet. The hall way was very plush with deep pile carpet and wide stairs leading to the upper floors. On the first floor landing an officer stood at the top of the stairs in full view from the hall and another stood outside the Central Recruitment office door or what there was left of it. The officer beckoned Palmer up. On the landing the first thing he saw was the splintered edge of the door and the broken lock littering the floor. He stepped over it and into a large open space modern office. The Chief Firearms Officer came out of the small kitchen alcove to the rear of the office.

'All clear Sir nobody in the place.'

Palmer pointed to the broken door. 'Hope you rang the bell first. That repair will come out of my budget.' He smiled knowingly at the officer.

'Sorry Sir but we don't like to let our targets know we are coming. We never know what kind of reception they might give us.'

'Quite right too, a shame she wasn't here. Bit of a damp squib really. Would have been nice to catch her quickly.' He turned to Gheeta. 'Sergeant we'd better get forensics down here and see what they can dig up. Can't see they'll get much but we had better go through the motions.' He turned back to the Chief Firearms Officer. 'I want this place sealed off. I'll leave a uniformed chap but I think I'd feel a lot better if you could spare one of your chaps to keep him company until forensics arrive just in case she comes back.'

'No problem Sir.'

'Right then, one down and one to go. Off to the Dolland's house and see if we have better luck there. Come on.'

Chapter 33

The Dolland's house was a very nice 1940's semi in
Harrow Hill. Palmer took the same procedure as at
Curzon Street. Two Firearms Officers went with him
and Sergeant Singh to the front door whilst a third
circled round the side entrance to cover the back in
the event of somebody deciding to make a hurried
exit that way. They didn't.
Mr Dolland was home and took them into the back
lounge. It was a bit pokey by today's standards but
quite adequate for a couple. Palmer left a plain
clothes man inside the front door. He hadn't asked for
uniformed officers on this one as should Mrs Dolland
arrive home and see one positioned outside the house
she would be off like a bat out of Hell.

   Having previously only had just run of the mill type
dealings with the Police in his job as Security
Manager at The Majestic Mr Dolland quickly grasped
that this was a more serious visit.

   'Well Chief Superintendent you don't come visiting
with firearms officers for an overdue parking ticket.
What have we done? I'm assuming it's to do with the
Recruitment Company, have we unknowingly placed
a terrorist cell into the Hotels? We do our best to
check references with the Home Office data bases but
you never know these days?'

   Palmer took off his trilby and sat down on an upright
table chair. Armchairs were available but with his
sciatica having a field day he felt more comfortable
on a firm base. He smiled reassuringly at Mr Dolland
who remained standing.

'Terrorists? No Sir nothing like that. You'd have a much heavier squad in your house if that were the case and I don't think I would have rung the bell. Is Mrs Dolland due home soon?'

'I really don't know she keeps irregular hours just like I do. The hotel business is a twenty four hour merry go round, if a staff member doesn't turn up she has to find an immediate replacement day or night. If you need to talk to her I can ring her mobile.' He made to reach a phone on a side table.

Palmer stopped him, 'I'd rather you didn't worry her. Do you know her plans for today? Where she is likely to be?'

Dolland was getting very aware that this police visit was centering around his wife and was, judging by the questions being asked, pretty serious. 'I really have no idea Chief Superintendent, would you like to tell me what all this about and then perhaps I can help you further?'

Palmer thought for a moment. This was no time to be worried about hurting Dolland's feelings or skirting round the problem so he took the bull by the horns. 'What was your wife's maiden name before you got married Sir?'

Dolland thought it a peculiar question. 'Robins.'

'Dorothy Robins?'

'Yes.'

'So where does the Evelyn name come from?'

'She hated the name Dorothy. People called her Dolly, Dotty or Dot so she used her middle name of Evelyn instead.'

'So Dorothy Robins became Evelyn Dolland.'

'Yes, I suppose that's right. Have we broken some obscure law?'

Palmer smiled. 'No not at all Sir.' He turned to Sergeant Singh. 'No wonder we couldn't find her.' He returned to Dolland. 'Do you know much about your wife's life before you met her Sir? I'm sorry to be so blunt but we are investigating a very serious case in which we suspect, indeed we know, your wife is heavily involved.'

Dolland was visibly shaken. Slowly he sat in an armchair 'Before I met her?'

'Yes Sir. Did you know she had a child from a previous marriage,' Palmer pitched straight in. No time to beat about the bush and worry about being diplomatic, 'a daughter named Angela?'

'Yes, yes I did. It was an awful time for her. The child took her own life after being bullied at College. An awful period in my wife's life, I don't think she ever really got over it.'

'You are probably right Sir.' Gheeta sensed relief in Palmer's voice that Angela was in the public domain. He continued. 'Let me bring you up to date…' Palmer relayed to Dolland the reason they were there, the murders and their relationship to the Child Poem and to the Milner College.

Dolland sat silent in disbelief trying to take in what he had just been told about his wife and make some sense out of it.

Palmer broke the silence speaking softly. 'We do need to find your wife Sir. She may think she's untouchable and not on our radar as she's been able to get away with the killings so far and sometimes that can effect a killer's mind and they escalate their field

of murder to outside their original motivation. Do
you have any idea as to where she might be? It would
be very helpful. Even the slightest inclination?'

'She'll be at that College.' It was a firm immediate
response.

'At the Milner College?'

'Yes.'

'What makes you think that sir?'

'She never spoke about the girls involved in the
bullying, never. I had no idea she even knew who
they were. But when other so called 'celebrities'
came on the telly, ones that she knew had been to that
College she would always say *I'll burn that place to
the ground one day*.' She must have said that so many
times.'

Palmer and Singh were already up and halfway out
of the room.

Palmer donned his trilby on the way. 'Thank you
Mister Dolland. I'll leave a uniformed officer with
you and my Sergeant will put victim's support in
touch with you, I think you might benefit from their
counselling.' He felt genuinely sorry for Dolland, not
every day you learn your wife is a serial killer.
Sergeant Singh got on her mobile and organised back
up as they sped, sirens screaming towards Red Post
Hill and the College.

Chapter 34

'It's empty Sir? Nobody here,' Sergeant Singh looked around the empty forecourt of the College as they got out of the squad car, 'Must be holiday time.' They had positioned the two local back-up Officers who were at the College entrance when they arrived to stay at the gate and gone in with the Firearms Officers.

'Looks like it Sergeant,' Palmer said as he scanned the buildings for life, 'I think you must be right there should be a caretaker here though shouldn't there, a place this size can't be without somebody here all the time surely?'

'That principal we met, Timms-Beddis, he has a flat here somewhere Sir,' Gheeta said as she mounted the steps to the front door and looked at the bells. 'His name's on a bell guv.' She pushed it, they waited, nothing.

'Try again.' Palmer shielded his eyes from the sun as he stood back and looked up at the front windows on the upper floors. There was still no answer to the bell. He turned to the two firearms officers standing beside their transit. 'You two hang on here whilst we take a look around the back.' He motioned Singh to follow him and set off round the corner of the building.

'Have you got that accounts lady's number on your mobile, the one who works here?'

'Yes guv Miss Jacobs, shall I give her a call and get her down here?'

'I think so. We need to get inside and Timms 'what's-his-name' might be away on holiday himself. Tell her to bring the keys. If we break in the alarms will go off.'

'If they've got any guv.'

'They must have surely.'

Gheeta gave Miss Jacobs a call. She was in. She lived locally and would come straight away. Gheeta used her radio to let the Firearms Officers know to expect her and let her through.

The main building was a large one as you would expect for a College housing a theatre and rehearsal rooms. The side path was a good sixty yards long and when they reached the next corner they turned it and found themselves at the rear of the main block in an open gravelled square with two warehouse style tall buildings on two of its sides and the third side opening onto a playing field. The ground floor windows of the buildings were bricked up.

All was quiet. But their attention was drawn to the tallest of the two buildings, a six story warehouse where the ground floor door was stood wide open outwards to the square. From their position forty yards away they could see the open door was steel reinforced on the inside.

'Strange that isn't it?' Palmer nodded towards the door.

'Doesn't look like it's been forced guv, maybe Timms-Beddis or somebody is inside working?'

'He didn't strike me as the type of bloke to be doing a bit of maintenance.'

They made their way across the square their footsteps crunching on the gravel. As they got to about twenty yards from the door a distraught Timms-Beddis staggered and stumbled out of it falling head first onto the gravel where he lay shaking and moaning. Behind him Evelyn Dolland , a large knife in her hand, stood for a moment in the doorway she had pushed him out of before she leant forward and pulled it shut with loud steel bang followed by the grating sound of steel security bolts being slid into position.

'Jesus Christ!' It took a second for Palmer and Singh to realise what had happened and then they raced to Timms-Beddis and turned him onto his back. Gheeta called in the others on her radio and put out a call for any available back-up in the vicinity to attend before ripping the blood soaked shirt sleeve off Timms-Beddis and tying it tightly around his upper arm to try and staunch the blood coming from a deep cut on his forearm. He was obviously in deep shock and fear, shaking uncontrollably.

'She stabbed me,' he blurtled out between sobs. 'Stabbed me….I'll die…. She stabbed me, said she wanted the keys to store building….I wouldn't give them to her and she stabbed me.'

'Calm down Sir you won't die it's only a surface cut,' Palmer lied as he could plainly see it was down to the bone. 'The Doctor's on his way, we'll soon have you patched up.'

The firearms officers arrived. One knelt with his pistol aimed up at the windows of the warehouse above them.

'Christ…what happened here Sir?' asked number two.

Palmer was quite calm. Gheeta had noticed this before in her boss. When the shit really hit the fan his mind became clear, his orders precise and correct and he gave the aura of being in total control which of course, he was. He had faced many similar situations in his career and his experience in them had formulated a clear procedure to be taken when such things occur.

'Our target is inside. She's armed with a knife and she is very, very dangerous.' The sound of sirens announced the arrival of some back up at the front of the main building as he spoke. 'You two go round the back of this building and check any back doors and ground floor windows in case she makes a run for it that way. But, remember, she is very, very dangerous. She's not armed but if the knife comes out then taser her immediately. If it all goes belly up you have my authority to use your weapons. That's an order okay?'

They both nodded and were gone as half a dozen uniformed officers from the local Camberwell and Peckham stations came round the corner of the main building and across the courtyard to join Palmer and Singh.

Gheeta was on her radio again ordering up an ambulance for Timms-Beddis who seemed to have calmed down considerably after being told he wasn't going to die.

Palmer quickly told the uniformed boys his and Sergeant Singh's names, their Squad details, why they were there and what had happened. He had two of them lift Timms-Beddis and cart him away to await the medics and seal off the entrance from the road with the Officers already there. Last thing he wanted was the nosey public making a nuisance of themselves.

'Guv…' Gheeta pointed to the steel door. Smoke could be seen creeping out from the top of it. She clicked on her radio again and asked for the fire brigade to attend. Quickly.

Palmer looked at the smoke. 'Dolland said that his wife had said she would burn the place down. It looks like she's keeping her word everybody back to the other side of the square. We don't know what's inside that building. This place is an art college so could be all sorts of pyrotechnics.' They all moved back to a safe distance. 'Give the firearms boys a call and see if they can see anything round the back.'

They couldn't. There was a back door to the building but it was shut and solid. No ground floor windows. But they could see smoke seeping out of the first and second floor windows. There was a steel zig-zag fire escape with doors off to each of the six floors. Should they try and get inside from one of them?

'No,' was Palmer's strong reply.

The fire was quickly taking hold. Red and bright yellow flames could be seen through the first and second floor windows which were beginning to crack and fall out with the heat.

Palmer was starting to feel the heat from the building too and was worried. 'Unless she gets to the fire escape at the back she's not going to get out of there.'

Gheetas radio beeped. She took the message. 'Miss Jacobs has arrived Sir.'

'Bring her round.'

Gheeta relayed the message and a minute later a shocked looking Miss Jacobs arrived in the company of a uniformed officer.

She held her hand to her mouth in horror at the scene. 'Oh My God….Oh My God….what happened?'

Palmer gave her one of his calm down it's under control smiles although he knew it was not. 'The fire brigade are on their way but we need to know what that building is used for, what's inside it?'

Miss Jacobs seemed mesmerised her eyes didn't leave the building. 'Props, I mean everything, everything we need to run the College and teach the students…..theatre props, costumes, cameras, machines, control desks, back drops, everything. Oh My God this will finish us.'

'Is there anything in there that might explode, stage pyrotechnics, fireworks?'

'No not allowed by law. They are in a separate secure shed at the end of the playing field.' She pointed across to the field.

'Good.' Palmer was relieved.

'Oh My God! The cylinders are in there, the gas cylinders.'

'The what?'

'Propane gas cylinders. The heating in the theatre and rehearsal rooms is very old and inadequate so we supplement it with gas fires. We don't have gas in the building, all electric so we use bottled gas. They should be kept outside but we had so many stolen Timms-Beddis stores them inside there.'

The fire was now plainly in charge. The heat from the flames licking out of the broken windows was becoming uncomfortable for them a good forty yards distance away.

The existence of gas cylinders inside was a real worry to palmer. 'Right then, you lot back round the corner out of sight of the building please. If those cylinders go up one of them could come across here at the speed of light and take you out.'

They all moved round the corner to safety leaving Palmer and Singh. The sound of the fire tenders approaching could be heard.

'They won't get down that drive guv too narrow,' Gheeta was crouched next to Palmer looking at the windows for any sight of Mrs Dolland, 'have to run the hoses from the road and that's going to take time.'

'Chief Superintendent!' It was Miss Jacobs peering round the corner and calling.

Palmer waved her back shouting. 'Miss Jacobs please get out of sight.'

'I will but I thought you ought to know about that building,' she was having to shout above the noise of cracking timber and splintering glass.

'What about it?'

'It's the one that the girl jumped from. The sixth floor corner window.' She pointed up to the window and ducked back out of sight just as the first two gas cylinders exploded loudly inside the building followed by a rumble as a floor and masonry collapsed.

'Dolland's not going to get out of there guv and we can't do anything can we.' It was a statement not a question.

'No nothing, we can't do a bloody thing. Oh Christ…. look.'

Gheeta followed his gaze up to the sixth floor corner window. It was getting blackened from the smoke inside but the outline of a figure desperately banging fists against it could be seen.

'She won't be able to open it,' Miss Jacobs was back poking her head round the corner and looking up, 'they're all double glazed and locked. Oh my God she'll burn alive in there.'

Another scuffle behind them and some shouting announced the arrival of Mr Bennett trying unsuccessfully to escape the clutches of two officers holding him back.

'What's he doing here? Let him through!' Palmer ordered and Bennett joined them crouching against the wall. He offered his explanation before Palmer could ask.

'She rang me just as my solicitor got me bailed out. Said she was here and to come over. She didn't say she'd set the place alight.'

'You knew what she was doing all along didn't you,' Palmer shouted above the crackling of the burning building. 'She rang you after every murder didn't she, we have the phone records.'

'Yes, yes of course she did.....if she was caught I was going to continue until they were all dead. But she did it didn't she....she got our dear Angela's revenge. Where is she have you arrested her?'

'She's in there.' Palmer shouted above the crackling and banging from the inferno.

A steel pole smashed through the sixth floor corner window as Evelyn Dolland frantically tried to escape the flames licking up behind her. There was only one way out. Bennett looked up to the window as the glass fell and shattered on the ground.

'Oh God she's going to jump! Evelyn don't ...wait!' he shouted. 'WAIT!' And made to run across the gravel towards the building but Palmer had his arm held tightly.

Up at the broken window Dolland used the steel pole to hit at the jagged glass edges around the window frame to make a large enough escape hole and began to pull and push herself through, her clothes in flames and the jagged glass cutting them and her as she emerged slowly.

'She's going to jump guv!' Gheeta's panic shout was made as Mr Bennett got away from Palmer's grip and hobbled blindly through the swirling smoke towards the building in the vain and stupid hope that he might catch her.

Without thinking both Palmer and Singh went after him. Palmer made it first his sciatic pain in the leg dulled by the surge of adrenalin coursing through his body. It was a futile and stupid effort to pull Bennett out of the way of the plunging, flame engulfed body of his first wife which hit the pair of them and the ground with equal force.

Chapter 35

Mrs P poured Gheeta a cup of tea in the Palmer kitchen and sat down to the table beside her.

'Such a stupid man, I told him to take the retirement package they offered last time but he won't! He won't hear of it, says he'd be bored rigid pottering around at home all day. I said he could join clubs and he said his squad was his club and he didn't want anymore.'

'He'd be missed Mrs P. I'd really miss him and I know the team would. Not many like your husband left in the force.'

'No, and very nearly one less wasn't there, fancy trying to catch that falling lady, stupid man.' She shook her head in disbelief.

'It was all very spur of the moment Mrs P. sort of immediate reaction…we just ran after Bennett, I don't think the governor was trying to catch the lady. He just wanted to get Mister Bennett out of the danger.'

'You had more sense.'

'Probably not…I was just slower off the mark. Anyway that was all two weeks ago how is he doing?'

'Leg in plaster, arm in plaster and a sling …and damn miserable with it.'

'Miserable?'

'He wants to get back to the Yard, back to work….doctor says another week before the plaster comes off and he can walk normally again so you've another week of peace.'

'Be good to have him back, we do miss him.'

'So would the family if he'd been killed.' Tears welled up in Mrs P's eyes.

'Don't say that.' Gheeta reached across and pressed her hand.

Mrs P composed herself. 'Well, he's got a large family and sometimes I think he's got to slow down and give them more time. The Met would still function if Justin took the holiday time he's entitled to. Seems that every time we decide to take a holiday some serial killer pops up and ruins it. He's had one Christmas Day at home in the last eight. He'd only seen little George twice before this accident.'

'It's a funny thing Mrs P but being in the police is a bit like being in a large family. My mum thinks I'm married to the force. Can't explain it but it gets into your blood. It's a drug.'

Mrs P put a hand on Gheeta's shoulder. 'I know, I knew I'd be competing with it when I married him. And I know that sometimes he worries that he hasn't given me as much time as he ought.' She smiled. 'But he has. I tell him that I wouldn't want it any other way. Our family is built on a rock Gheeta, and that rock is Justin. But don't tell him I said so.' They both laughed.

Gheeta got serious. 'You know Mrs P. I was thinking about the case on the way over here. The whole Bennett family wiped out because of revenge and five other families mourning the loss of a loved one. Doesn't make sense does it? Nobody wins, everybody loses. If one of *your* family was really hurt or even murdered by somebody would you take revenge Mrs P?'

'No.'

'No?'

'I wouldn't have to, Justin would kill them,' she smiled, 'and with his experience he'd probably get away with it. Give me your cup I'll make a fresh one and you can go and bring him up to date with all the office scandal. He's in the lounge watching telly.'

Chapter 36

In the lounge Palmer was indeed watching telly. But not the Barcelona game he wanted to watch on Sky 'catch up'. His leg and arm in plaster prevented him from bending far enough to reach the remote which lay on the floor where Daisy the dog had knocked it as she made herself comfortable on the sofa next to Palmer. So the TV had auto-tuned into the last channel Mrs P had been on last night. Skype…and who was already on it…Benji…

'Oh hello Justin, how are you today…I was just going to chat to my pal in France but you popped up so I thought I'd say hello …..you been drinking?.... you look plastered to me! Hee hee…get it? plastered…. just a little joke…you look a lot better…anyway I need to talk to Mrs P. about her dahlia tubers, time to think about lifting them and storing. You need some dry sand and a cool place in the garden shed… I cut back my Syringa yesterday did you notice from your upstairs windows….well it was getting a bit straggly…..and your Wisteria is just divine, mine has been a disappointment this year probably the late frosts.......did I tell you about the mole I had in my lawn….well I looked out and I thought a dog had got in and dug a hole, not your Daisy of course… I do love your daisy…she's so gentle….anyway when I got out to look at it ……….'
He carried on unaware that Gheeta had come into the room, seen the situation and picked up the remote out of sight of the Skype web cam. She held it towards Palmer but kept it just out of his reach.

'I was thinking that Detective *Inspector* Singh has a nice ring to it guv.'

Palmer smiled. 'If that Sky Sports channel isn't on in ten seconds young lady it's more likely to be *Constable* Singh.'

THE END.

The Author

B.L.Faulkner was born into a family of petty
criminals in Herne Hill, South London and attended
the first ever comprehensive school in the UK,
William Penn in Peckham and East Dulwich where he
attained no academic qualifications other than GCE
'O' levels in Art and English and a Prefect's badge!
(some say he stole all three!)

His mother had great theatrical aspirations for young
Faulkner and pushed him into auditioning for the
Morley Academy of Dramatic Art at the Elephant and
Castle where he was accepted but only lasted 3
months before being asked to leave as no visible
talent had surfaced. Mind you, during his time at the
Academy he was called to audition for the National
Youth Theatre by Trevor Nunn...50 years later he's
still waiting for the call back!

His early writing career was as a copy writer with the
advertising agency Erwin Wasey Ruthrauff & Ryan
in Paddington during which time he got lucky with
some light entertainment scripts sent to the BBC and
Independent Television and became a script editor
and writer on a freelance basis working on most of
the LE shows of the 1980-90s. During that period,
whilst living out of a suitcase in UK hotels for a lot of
the time, he filled many notebooks with Palmer case
plots and in 2016 finally found time to start putting
them in order and into book form. Six are finished
and published so far, more to come. He hopes you

enjoy reading them as much as he enjoyed writing them.

Find out more about B.L.Faulkner and the *real* UK major heists and robberies including the Brinks Mat robbery and the Hatton Garden Heist plus the gangs and criminals that carried them out including the Krays and the Richardsons on his crime blog at *geezers2016@wordpress.com*

Take care and thank you for buying this book. An honest review would be very much appreciated if you have time and there are more Palmer books to read if you like the old s*d!

ps...No, I didn't pursue the family business of petty crime.....honest.

Printed in Great Britain
by Amazon